The Playboy and The Single Mum

Alexia Adams

Copyright

The Playboy and The Single Mum
(Vintage Love Book Two)

By Alexia Adams

This is a work of fiction. Names, characters, corporations, institutions, organizations, events, or locales in this novel are either the product of the author's imagination or, if real, used fictitiously. The resemblance of any character to actual persons (living or dead) is entirely coincidental.

Published by:
Alexia Adams
Suite 377
255 Newport Drive
Port Moody, BC V3H 5H1
Canada

Contact: Alexia@alexia-adams.com
www.alexia-adams.com

Edited by Julie Sturgeon
Cover design by Steven Novak

Ebook ISBN 978-0-9939126-2-7
Print ISBN 978-1-9991756-9-6

First Ebook Edition April 2016
First Print Edition October 2020

Product of Canada

Dedication

In memory of Jules Bianchi. #17 Forever.

Acknowledgements

This book would not be readable without the amazing talent of my editor, Julie. And it wouldn't have been possible without the fascinating world of Formula 1. To the drivers, team principals, aerodynamicists, mechanics, and everyone who works in the background, thank you for putting on a spectacular show. F1 has been my favorite sport since childhood when I used to watch it with my dad. I've wanted to write a story centered around Formula 1 for years and am so happy I finally managed to find two characters willing to go through the intense highs and lows of race season.

Finally, I'd like to acknowledge the support of my family who pretend to understand when I forget to do something because I'm off, at least mentally, in some distant land. Thank you, too, to all my readers who keep buying my books and make living this wacky writer's dream possible. I hope you enjoy *The Playboy and The Single Mum*.

Chapter One

It was only eight in the morning and already Lexy wanted to start her day over. Of course, being awakened at five thirty by her three-year-old son with the news he had a tummy ache seconds before he threw up all over her was never the best way to begin a day. Thankfully, as soon as he'd vomited Max'd felt better and had toddled off to watch CBeebies while she showered, threw her bedding in the wash, and got them both ready for their respective days: His to the downstairs flat where Sonia looked after him while Lexy was at work, and hers to catch the Tube to her office in Victoria where she spent her time trying to sell crap to people who already had too much stuff. Ah, the joys of advertising.

She was about to fall asleep on her forty-minute commute when the front page article of the paper the man across from her was reading caught her attention. Daniel Michaud, Formula 1 driver and the face of her firm's biggest client, stared at her in all his masculine beauty. What the hell had he done now? She'd been the one to pitch him to Destin Designs as the perfect front man for that up-and-coming fashion house's luxury brand. He had specific behavior clauses in his contract. If he'd screwed up, she'd be the one to pay the price. Losing a 2.5 million-euro contract was probably nothing to the international playboy. Losing her job would be devastating to Lexy; she barely covered her bills now.

She tried to read the article from across the carriage, but as the train filled up and people stood in front of her, it proved impossible. Of course she couldn't read the story on her phone, because for some reason the London Underground had to remain the last bastion against technology, so there was still no mobile service available.

Finally, she reached Victoria station and rushed aboveground, only to find it was pouring rain. And she'd left her umbrella on the Tube. Typical. And, as with all rainy days in London, the city's fleet of taxicabs had dissolved into black puddles. No getting around it; she had to leg it to work in three-inch heels and a pencil skirt. Still, it was only four blocks—how wet could she get?

Turned out, very wet.

"Is it raining?" Tori, the receptionist, asked as Lexy squelched across the marble-tiled floor. There was enough water in her shoes to bathe Max.

"No, I thought I'd switch it up and shower after I dressed today," Lexy replied as she pushed a dripping strand of hair behind her ear. Chirpy Australians were just too much to take some days.

"And a happy Tuesday morning to you, sweetie. To further make your day, Mr. Petersen wants to see you as soon as you get in."

Oh God, this wasn't good. There was only one reason the head of the company would want to see her on a morning when he normally didn't get in until noon. She was about to get fired. Well, she wasn't going down in this state. She had some pride.

"Give me ten minutes before you tell him I'm here," Lexy begged.

"What's it worth?"

"I'll cover the reception desk for an extra half hour on Friday so you can meet your boyfriend for lunch in Docklands."

"You're on. Oh, and here." Tori tossed her a plastic shopping bag. "I was going to return this to the store because it was too small, but looks like you could use it. Girl, if you're going to wear a white top and get drenched, you should at least put on a nice bra. That one looks like it was left over from your breastfeeding days."

It was. She'd been so busy with her final assignment for her online university class that she hadn't done laundry in two weeks. She peeked inside the bag. A light turquoise top lay at the bottom. "Thanks, Tori. I owe you."

"Remember that when Daniel Michaud arrives. I expect an introduction."

"Daniel Michaud is coming here?" *Could my day get any worse?*

"He's expected in around noon. I have a car at City Airport ready to pick him up when his private jet lands."

"Have you read the story? What's he done?"

"Some other guy's wife, apparently."

Lexy groaned. The top of the list of forbidden

behavior. At least she'd get the chance to kick him in the privates for getting her fired. "Thanks for the shirt."

Lexy fled to the women's washroom to survey the damage. So not good. Her mascara had run and irritated her eyes, so she'd have to wear her glasses now. Her hair was plastered to her head, and there wasn't a dry spot anywhere on her clothes.

She needed a miracle. Preferably one that would occur in the next ten minutes.

What she got was a pathetic hand dryer and some wipes she kept in her bag to clean Max's endlessly sticky fingers. Oh God, she couldn't lose her job, as miserable as it was. She had to provide for Max and keep his father from finding out their son even existed.

There was a sharp knock on the door and Tori stuck her head around. "Thought you might need this, too," she said, handing over a Marks & Spencer bag.

Lexy pulled out a super-sexy bra. "Um, why?"

"Because I refuse to allow you to wear that nice top with that ugly thing you've got on. And you need the confidence of a good sheepdog bra."

Lexy shook her head. Anyone who tried to have more than a two-minute conversation with the antipodean receptionist would come away with the firm conviction that English and Australian were two entirely different languages. "Dare I ask?"

"Rounds 'em up and points 'em in the right direction." Tori grabbed her own breasts and demonstrated.

I'm getting fired with perky boobs. But she had to admit it did help in the confidence department. And if she fell on her face, there'd be something to cushion the impact.

"Mr. Petersen called again to see if you'd come in yet. So you'd better get a wiggle on. And good luck," Tori called out with the door already closing behind her.

Tori was right: Lexy couldn't hide out in the bathroom all day. Time to face the music. She risked one more glance in the mirror. It was the best she could do. She'd pulled her hair back into a tight bun and put on red lipstick to make up for the fact that she wore no other makeup. Thankfully, her skirt had dried somewhat by using the hand dryer. How presentable did one need to be to get sacked?

Daniel Michaud had better hope she was out of the building by the time he arrived. Or he'd be driving his next race with one less functioning testicle.

"Alexandra, please come in," Mr. Petersen said as she hovered by his door. His secretary obviously hadn't expected him in so early either and wasn't at her desk yet. Her boss was one of three people who always used her full name, rejecting the diminutive Lexy. Her ex-husband and her father were the other two. She didn't care much for them, either.

"You wanted to see me, Mr. Petersen?" Dumb question. Maybe she should have had a second coffee this morning. And a sausage buttie. It was definitely a sausage buttie kind of day.

"Have you seen the papers?"

"No, unfortunately, I haven't. Has something happened?" She widened her eyes and let her bottom lip fall open. Her son Max got away with mischief by playing the sweet innocent; she'd give it a try.

"Daniel Michaud has breached the terms of his contract. It is too late in the ad campaign to get another face. But this can't be allowed to happen again. So the CEO of Destin Designs and I have decided that Michaud needs a minder."

Yes! She wasn't going to be fired. They just needed her to come up with someone to keep a sexy playboy in control. She ran through a list of possible candidates in her head, ready to suggest a name as soon as Mr. Petersen stopped looking at her with that odd expression.

He cleared his throat. "You will accompany Mr. Michaud for the rest of the F1 season. Make sure he doesn't get into any more trouble."

"Mr. Petersen, I can't. Have you forgotten I have a son? I can't leave him for two months."

"I'm sure you can come to some sort of arrangement for him. Our client is willing to pay 20,000 pounds for you to secure childcare for the next two months. Further, if the campaign is successful and Mr. Michaud behaves in a manner as outlined in the contract, you will be given a bonus of 50,000 pounds. I'm sure that's a sweet enough deal to put up with two months without your son. Besides, you can see him between races."

"All the remaining F1 races are abroad. The European season is over. I appreciate your generous offer, but I'm sure we can find someone else suitable."

"The fact that you know where the remaining races

are is proof that you are the ideal candidate, Alexandra."

She was drowning in quicksand, reaching for anything to stop herself going under. "There has to be someone else."

"Name me one person who first knows the Formula 1 circus as well as you. You were practically born on the track. And second, speaks fluent French, as well as, what? Two other languages?"

"Four. Italian, Spanish, German, and Russian." Languages she'd picked up trailing her father around the Formula 1 races for the first five years of her life. Mr. Petersen had described it accurately: it *was* a circus. One she'd put far behind her.

"Point three: you have a degree in psychology. You can get inside his head and keep him on the straight and narrow."

"I haven't completed my degree yet."

"Doesn't matter. I'm sure you know enough. He drives a car for a living and has a different woman in his bed every night. How deep can he be?"

Not as deep as she was sinking. "But the whole idea behind the advertising campaign is for him to be seen as an international playboy with a woman in every city. If I'm trailing him around, won't it look like we're dating? The media may start to think I'm his girlfriend," she said.

Mr. Petersen didn't even bother to look her up and down. "You're not his type. And no disrespect, but I don't think anyone would confuse you for a WAG."

No, she was the antithesis of a sports celebrity wife

or girlfriend. With her frizzy hair and high-street clothes, no one would mistake her for a woman able to attract a celebrity. And given Daniel's love 'em and leave 'em philosophy, she was fine with that.

"Still, don't you think a man would be better for the job?"

"No. But that brings us to point four. You were the one who recommended Daniel Michaud for this advertising campaign. You convinced the client he was the only one who had the right image. If this goes wrong, then it's your head on the chopping block. That should be motive enough for you to do a good job."

"But … I …" There was nothing else to say. She *was* the best person for the job. It was just that she didn't want it. Babysitting a spoiled playboy millionaire racecar driver who went through women like her son went through Cheerios was not her idea of career advancement.

"He'll be here soon. Let me speak to him first then I'll call you in. In the meantime, sort out your childcare. Be ready to leave when he tells you."

And with that, her world imploded. Yep, definitely a day she'd like to start over.

***

Daniel ground his teeth. *What am I, some kind of errant schoolboy summoned to the headmaster's office?* He should never have signed the damn contract. He knew the behavior clause was going to bite him in the ass one day. And the whole thing was just a stupid misunderstanding. Sure, he'd been photographed carrying his ex-girlfriend, now the wife of another man, out of his hotel room while wearing only his boxers. But it was all innocent. Too bad he couldn't tell anyone the truth, because it would reveal Jacqueline's secret. And he'd never do that.

So instead he had to play the penitent playboy and promise not to get in any more "trouble." A couple of demure smiles, a firm handshake, maybe a few drinks, then he'd be good to go. Back to Paris for a few days, or maybe he'd lay low at his brother's chateau in the Loire Valley. Then off to Russia for the next race.

The championship was tight again this year. He needed to win the majority of the last remaining five races to clinch the title. Or for his two closest competitors to not finish a race. He never relied on luck, though. He wanted to win by skill, show the world that his first championship hadn't been a fluke or because his car was better than anyone else's. Last year he'd missed winning it all by two points. He had to be the best this year. His career was all he had left.

"Did you fly straight in from Japan, sir?" the driver asked as they stopped at a light.

"Yes." Thankfully he had his brother's private plane, complete with a double bed so he'd been able to sleep some of the way. He'd given a lift to four mechanics who had celebrated the team's one-two placing, so it had been noisy until they'd passed out.

"Good race," the driver continued. "Shame about the pit stop. You should've come in first."

Daniel forced his media relations smile. "Everyone

did their best. At least the team got both top spots." And narrowed the margin between him and his teammate. Robert was catching up—only ten points separated them now; the difference between first and third place. Daniel clenched his hands. The wait between races was the worst. Gave a man too much time to think.

He leaned his head back and shut his eyes, hoping the chauffeur would take the hint. It wasn't that he didn't appreciate his fans. But it had been a tough weekend, followed by an epically long flight. All he wanted was some peace and quiet for a few hours. Was that too much to ask?

"Sir, we're here." The driver's voice penetrated the light doze into which he'd fallen.

Daniel scrubbed his hands over his face, wishing he'd taken the time to shave as well as brush his teeth. He took a deep breath and stepped from the vehicle.

Showtime.

The receptionist's eyes ate him up like he was a chocolate éclair at a dieting convention. He flashed his trademark smile and leaned casually against her desk. "*Bonjour*. I am Daniel; Mr. Petersen is expecting me." He could speak English with very little accent, but most women seemed to prefer it when he laid on the French charm.

A flush crept up the woman's neck as she nodded then dialed a number on her desk phone, announcing his arrival. He didn't miss the small sigh that escaped her lips as he left the room with Mr. Petersen.

The boardroom where he was taken had glass walls

on three sides, like being in a fish bowl. The two men already at the table, however, were more like snarling dogs.

Become the face of Destin Designs, they said. It'll be fun, they said. All you have to do is get your photo taken with gorgeous women dripping off you, wear their clothes, which he had to admit were rather nice, and rake in the money. Not that he needed the money. He made plenty as a driver, and his brother had invested it wisely so Daniel could live off the interest. But the proceeds from this contract were earmarked for something special. And he wanted it kept entirely secret.

"Daniel, so good of you to come when we called," Mr. Petersen said as he took the seat offered.

Like I had a choice.

"Gentlemen," Daniel began, "this whole thing with Jacqueline Lefebre is just a misunderstanding. There was no wrongdoing. You can ask her husband if you don't believe me." He shot his famed charming smile around the table, but for once it fell flat.

"Your contract with our client specifically states that you cannot be caught in an indiscretion with a married woman. It's one thing to be a playboy, another entirely to be a marriage-wrecker," one of the other men said, the one with the nose hairs almost touching his upper lip.

If they'd shot a rocket up his ass they couldn't have riled him more. He had no desire to get married, but he had great respect for those who chose to do so. He'd just as soon never drive again as destroy someone's relationship. But getting angry now wasn't going to help the situation. He forced the ire down and put ice in his words.

"Jacqueline is a friend. We've known each other for many years, even before her marriage." His jaw ached, trying to keep the smile on his face.

Mr. Petersen spread his arms wide. He was obviously trying to act as the reconciler in this meeting. "If there was nothing wrong, then issue a statement to the press explaining why you were carrying her out of your room in the middle of the night in a state of undress."

"No." Daniel sat back in his chair, waiting for the explosion. He wasn't disappointed.

"No?" Nose-hair guy slammed his fist on the table.

"It's not my story to tell. And the press has no right to know what goes on in my life once I'm off track."

"The contract—"

He stood, ready to leave. "Screw your contract. Rip it up. Fire me. Go on." He didn't need to take this crap from men whose idea of risk was to use a sand wedge to tee off in their weekly golf game.

"Now, now, Daniel, no need to make any hasty decisions," Mr. Petersen said. "We've come up with a solution to our little situation." How quickly it had gone from indiscretion to situation.

Daniel narrowed his eyes and tried to read Mr. Petersen's body language as he fiddled with his pen and avoided Daniel's gaze. Didn't take a genius to work out that Daniel wasn't going to like their *solution*. "What is it?"

"Well, we thought if you had someone to guide you a little more, remind you of our client's expectations, help you manage the media, that sort of thing, we could avoid any additional instances like the one that just occurred. Only until the race season is over, of course."

"You're getting me a … what do you British call them—a nanny? Someone to slap my wrist when I'm naughty, and give me an extra biscuit when I'm good?" Daniel was pretty sure steam was about to come out of his ears. They had to be kidding.

"She'll be discrete, just hanging around in the background, guiding you when need be. She won't interfere in your life. Unless you're about to make another error in judgment."

She? Probably some near-pensioner they wanted to give a little holiday to before retirement.

"And who is this woman who is to be my shadow conscience?"

Mr. Petersen swiveled in his chair and reached for the phone on the credenza behind him. "Alexandra, please come in now," he said.

Daniel scrubbed his hands over his face and closed his eyes. This was so freaking unbelievable. He needed to get some rest, then join his team and go over the modifications for the race in Russia.

The conference room door clicked open, and he lifted his protesting eyelids. Hot damn. He'd obviously fallen asleep and was dreaming. Because there was no way these three past-their-prime men could think that the minx before him was going to keep him in line.

Either that or they'd discovered his kryptonite. The woman standing hesitantly in the doorway had 'sexy librarian' written all over her. Her hair was pulled back severely and huge horn-rimmed glasses framed her molten chocolate eyes. And not even a wine barrel could hide that figure. She had curves that would require shifting into second gear to negotiate successfully.

When his eyes eventually returned to her face, the adoration he normally saw from women was decidedly absent. He walked around the table and held his hand out to her. Up close she was even more beautiful.

Reluctantly she put her hand in his. But rather than shake it, he raised it to his lips and kissed the back. "*Enchanté*, Alexandra."

He expected a little sigh, maybe a feminine giggle. Instead he got, "Oh, for God's sake," as she snatched her hand back.

He leveled his most charming smile at her. And crashed. What, were his lips broken today? He was seriously off his game. If this form carried over to his career, he could wave the championship goodbye. Her eyes spat fire at him. She clearly wasn't happy with her new assignment.

He, on the other hand, was intrigued by this enigma. The next two months were going to be very interesting indeed.

Chapter Two

It was so very wrong for one man to be that incredibly gorgeous and sexy. She'd expected that up close she'd be able to see some flaw, at least a pimple or two that got airbrushed out of the final photographs. But nothing. The man was perfection. It wasn't fair.

And when his lips touched the back of her hand… No wonder he had women falling at his feet. Imagine if those lips were anyplace more sensitive, say, working their way from her collarbone to her ear before venturing to her own lips.

"Oh, for God's sake."

From the startled looks on the faces of the four men, she'd said the words out loud. Shit. She didn't know whether to be angrier with herself for her reaction to what must be his normal way to greet a woman, or him for putting her in this awkward position.

The phone clutched in her left hand began to play the Winnie the Pooh theme song. She didn't need to look at her screen to know it was Sonia. Her friend hadn't answered earlier when Lexy called, and for a panicked moment she'd worried that Max was sicker than she'd thought and they were on their way to the hospital. Except she knew Sonia would have contacted her if that had happened. “Excuse me; this call is urgent. I have to take it,” she said before fleeing the room.

It might be bad behavior to run out just after being introduced to someone, but what were they going to do? Fire her? At the moment that would be a safer option than sequestering her with Daniel Michaud for eight weeks.

“Hey, Sonia, just give me a sec to find someplace private.”

Lexy scurried into an empty office and shut the door behind her. Sonia was her last hope to get out of this crazy scheme. If her friend couldn’t look after Max, there was no one else to do it, and therefore no way Lexy could leave.

“Max is fine, Lexy; no need to worry,” Sonia was quick to say. “We took the dog for a walk and the boys got muddy splashing in the puddles, so I threw them in the bath when we got home. That’s why I didn’t answer your call. Sorry if I worried you.”

“It’s not that. I, uh, I have to ask you something. Something huge.”

“What’s up? You know I’d do anything for you, hon.”

“My boss wants me to go on a business trip … for eight weeks, although I’ll probably be able to come back for a few days now and then. I completely understand if you can’t look after Max that long, especially with your baby due soon. But I could pay you twenty grand.”

Sonia burst into tears on the other end of the line. It

was too much to look after another rambunctious three-year-old when in the third trimester. How could Lexy even have asked?

"I'm sorry, Sonia. I didn't mean to upset you. I'll tell my boss I can't go." Relief and fear washed through her. She had an out, the perfect excuse not to spend two months in Daniel's intoxicating presence. But now she also had to find a new job.

"No, you've got it wrong," Sonia interjected. "Damn pregnancy hormones. I cry at toilet paper advertisements these days. You don't know how much you've just saved us. Of course we'll look after Max. You know we love him like our own. And when he's here Andrew behaves so much better, sometimes I think I should pay you." There was a muted sound at the other end as Sonia blew her nose. "Mark just called. He's been made redundant. We're already behind on the rent. I thought we'd have to move, and so close to the new baby coming. I was frantic. But the 20,000 will keep us going for months. Plus, if you're away, do you think my mum could stay in your flat? She's coming for the last month of my pregnancy to look after Andrew. If you're not going to be upstairs…"

"Of course your mum can stay at my place. But are you sure? I remember how exhausted I was when carrying Max." Exhausted, terrified, alone.

"Absolutely, and Mark and my mum will be here as well to help. Max will be fine. And it will give you a chance to be a woman for a change and not just a working mum. Maybe even have some fun."

Fun? She wouldn't recognize it if it slapped her in

the face—or kissed her hand in greeting. She took a deep breath. "If you're sure."

"I'm sure."

"Then I guess I'll tell my boss I can go."

At Sonia's end of the call she could hear two excited boys yell out, "Daddy, you're home!" Max's voice was as clear as Sonia's own son Andrew's. Lexy had tried several times to stop Max from calling Mark "Daddy." But Mark had said he didn't mind, and Andrew was happy to share his dad because Max didn't have one.

Max did have a dad. But he'd abandoned Lexy before she even knew she was pregnant, so she hadn't bothered to track him down and tell him he was a father. If he found out, would her ex-husband try to take her son from her? He was rich; he could provide Max with a life she could only dream about. But love was more important than money. Would the courts see it that way? She didn't want to test that assumption.

And with one of the remaining F1 races in Austin, Texas, she'd be right in Wesley's back yard. At least she wouldn't have Max with her. Even if she should run into her ex-husband, he needn't discover they had a son.

A shiver coursed down her spine and the coffee in her stomach churned.

Have fun? Not bloody likely.

Daniel stood again as she returned to the boardroom. Try as she might, she couldn't ignore his presence.

"Is everything okay?" he asked. "You ran out of

here like your house was on fire." There was genuine concern in his eyes. This would be so much easier if he stayed the arrogant international playboy. If he became a supportive man, one who stood at her side and encouraged her, she was in trouble.

"It's fine. I was just making some arrangements for this business trip." *Good. Keep it professional, Lexy.*

Daniel's gaze roved over her body again, an appreciative look in his eyes. No one had looked at her like that in a very long time. "Your husband or boyfriend doesn't object to you coming with me for eight weeks?"

"I have neither," she answered immediately. "I've sorted out what I needed to, so I'm good to go. When do you want me to join you? Russia's race is in two weeks. I guess you have to be there what, five days before?"

He blinked twice, and his mouth fell open at her comment. "Are you a fan?"

"Alexandra knows everything there is to know about Formula 1," Mr. Petersen interrupted. Her attention had been so absorbed by Daniel she'd forgotten her boss was still in the room. At least the two other men had left. "Her father is Gian-Franco Camparelli."

Daniel whistled, obviously impressed. Her father had been team principal at Ferrari during its most successful seasons. But it was probably his reputation as a Lothario that Daniel admired.

"My father and I haven't spoken in ten years," she said, crossing her arms. If he was thinking she had an in with the Ferrari team, she wanted to quash that dream right now.

Even Mr. Petersen looked uncomfortable at her vehemence. “Well, I’ll let you two sort out the details. Alexandra, stop by my office before you go. And you’ll need to speak with accounting, too, about where to deposit the 20,000.”

The older man shook hands with Daniel and gave her a wide berth before exiting the room.

“They’re paying you twenty grand to spend two months with me?”

“Hardly seems enough, does it?”

He laughed, the sound reverberating off the glass walls. Several people in cubicles outside peered in. She couldn’t repress her smile. At least he had a sense of humor.

Her smile disappeared, however, at his next words. “We need to get to know each other before we go to Russia. Once race week starts, I’m focused on the track. I won’t have time to give you the attention you deserve.”

“Let’s get one thing clear, *Monsieur* Michaud. I don’t want your attention. I’m to do a job—keep you out of trouble—nothing more.”

“Call me Daniel. Can we at least try to be friends? I’m not the ogre you imagine. Most people actually seem to like me.”

The danger was in liking him a little too much. But they were about to spend eight weeks together. It would be too exhausting to keep up this animosity. However, she’d keep her guard up. She’d been fooled by the "nice guy" routine once before. "All right. How soon do you want to get started? And where?"

His gaze caught hers and she lasted two seconds before she had to look away. She'd better stock up on heat-resistant underwear. This guy was hot enough to melt the cotton ones right off her.

"Can you be ready to leave in two days? I have to go up to Oxfordshire and rendezvous with my team. I'll be in meetings the whole time, and I promise to stay out of the press. We can meet at City Airport on Thursday afternoon and take my brother's plane to the Loire Valley. He has a house there we can stay in until we travel to Russia next week. I've just heard that my apartment in Paris is surrounded by paparazzi."

"I'll see you Thursday at two." She spun on her heel and left the room.

Forty-eight hours. Would that be long enough to etch into her brain that Daniel's smooth smile hid a womanizing heart?

***

Daniel scrolled through the messages on his phone while he waited for Alexandra in the private lounge at City Airport. He double checked, but no message from Jacques, his brother. If something had happened, surely he'd have heard about it.

Instead, his inbox was filled with questions about his relationship with Jacqueline and speculation about his love life. An ironic snort escaped. If the media knew he hadn't had a woman since before the season started

… but that didn't go with his carefully-crafted playboy persona, the very thing that had landed him in this predicament. His pretend womanizing had become so entrenched, even his brother believed it.

"Can I get you a drink, Mr. Michaud?" the lounge attendant asked.

He glanced up, forcing his trademark smile. "No, thanks. As soon as my travelling companion arrives, we'll be off."

If she arrived. Alexandra clearly hadn't wanted the assignment to chaperone him. *C'est des conneries.* He didn't need a minder. He needed to focus on his driving. Women had the power to destroy a racing career. And he was about to have one glued to his side for the next eight weeks.

"Well, if there's anything you need, anything at all, please let me know." With a disappointed smile, the attendant returned to her desk.

His finger hovered over the phone icon, tempted to call Alexandra. He could offer thirty grand for her to stay home and out of his life, pay back the advance, and walk away from the contract. Getting another sponsor wouldn't be a problem.

Except Grand-Papa hadn't raised a quitter or a coward. He'd meet his obligations, avoid getting too close to Alexandra, win the championship, and… And what? Spend the off-season in his apartment in Paris or his brother's empty chateau in the Loire? He scrubbed his hands over his face again. The restlessness that had kept him awake the past two nights was end-of-season nerves. Had to be.

His phone vibrated with an incoming message. Maybe Alexandra was canceling on him? Coming up with some lame excuse like she had to wash her hair? No, she was in advertising—it was bound to be way more inventive than that. He'd have to remember she was used to selling a product as well. Two phonies in a world of deception.

The message wasn't from her. It was from his alleged half brother, asking him to meet their father before the old man died of cancer. Daniel had decided long ago that his father was a loser who didn't live up to his responsibilities and he was better off without him. Then out of the blue earlier this year, he'd received a message from a Santiago Alvarez, claiming to be his relation. Evidently his father had just discovered Daniel existed and wanted to meet the son he'd never known about. Sounded like a con. The messages had become more frequent in the past six months, as his supposed father's cancer progressed and there was no hope of recovery.

As a celebrity, Daniel was no stranger to requests to meet, which usually included a desperate need for money at some point. So he hadn't bothered responding. Even if it were true, he'd managed without a father for twenty-eight years; he didn't need one now.

He was still staring at his phone when a delicate floral scent invaded his senses. He glanced up to see Alexandra less than a meter away, standing next to a large roller suitcase that had seen better days. She looked undeniably sad. *Merde.* He did not need to get involved in yet another woman's problems. Hadn't

Jacqueline's landed him in enough trouble?

Alexandra was dressed in a severe black trouser suit, the buttons of her white shirt done up to her neck. All business, all the time. What would it take to melt the ice princess?

"Ready?" he asked as he stood. He reached for her suitcase, and after a brief hesitation she let go of the handle.

She squared her shoulders and lifted her chin, a hint of a wobble in her voice. "Yes."

When finally they were seated in the leather chairs of the private jet, she looked around appreciatively. "Will we be traveling like this the whole time?"

At last a smile. He should be irritated that the trappings of luxury were what pleased her, but he was too relieved that she'd relaxed a bit. Which was stupid. It wasn't his job to make her happy.

"It's my brother's plane. So as long as he doesn't need it, I'm free to use it." He shrugged, hoping she didn't pursue the topic.

But she did. "Your brother is Jacques de Launay, right? I read he resigned as chairman of all his companies, and disappeared."

"Yes." His curt answer worked and she didn't ask any further questions. Even though it had been almost a year, he still wasn't used to the fact that Jacques and Grand-Papa weren't at home.

It was one of the reasons he was bringing Alexandra to the Loire. He hated going to the chateau with his family not there. It had always been his sanctuary, the place he could be himself. Now it was just a building, a reminder of a happy childhood. Still, he'd promised his brother that he'd check in periodically to make sure everything was okay.

At least it was still fully staffed. Jacques hadn't wanted anyone to lose their job when he made the decision to go into hiding with the woman he loved. They were probably bored out of their skulls with no family in residence. So when Daniel did show up, the staff fussed over him as if he were royalty.

Alexandra stared out the tiny window for the rest of the short flight. They sat less than a meter apart, but silence was a brick wall between them. A structure he'd built with his words. They'd have to find some rhythm, some common ground, or this was going to be an uncomfortable eight weeks. Tonight he'd ask the chef to make *steak au poivre,* he'd pop the cork on a premium bottle of wine, and see if he could get Alexandra to loosen up a bit.

Bertrand, the butler who doubled as a driver, was waiting for them when they landed. As the house came into view, Alexandra did a double take. "Holy crap, that's your brother's house?"

"*Oui*; welcome to Chateau de Vendee."

Bertrand stopped the car at the front door, and Daniel ushered Alexandra inside, out of the blustery rain. The housekeeper waited in the hallway. She wrapped him in a big hug before he'd even taken his coat off. "Welcome home," she said, kissing him on both cheeks.

Finally freed from her embrace, he gestured Alexandra forward. His guest was staring as though she'd just walked into Disneyland by mistake. He helped her out of her coat then introduced her. "Alexandra, this is Marie Dubois. Anything you need, she'll get it or make it for you."

Marie shook hands stiffly with Alexandra, becoming once more the formal staff member and not the warm hug she'd been to him since he'd been abandoned by his own mother at the age of three. The housekeeper took their wet coats from him and hurried from the hallway.

"I thought she was your mother from the way she greeted you," Alexandra said as Marie left.

"I wish. Marie was more a mother than the woman who gave birth to me. That cold-hearted cow lives in Paris and is banned from ever coming to this house again."

"Oh." Alexandra looked startled, as though this fantasyland had just become a pit of vipers. He needed to be careful that she didn't see behind his mask and discover all his secrets.

"Come into the *petit salon*. Marie will bring coffee and tea to us there." He led the way, resisting the urge to take her hand.

"Wow, this room is gorgeous," she said.

He was still impressed with the transformation the room had gone through. "My sister-in-law decorated it. Just before she … left."

Alexandra turned puzzled eyes on him. Then she spotted the oil portrait of him, Jacques, and his grandfather. She walked toward it as though in a trance.

"My brother and grandfather. Well, he's not really

my grandfather, but as he raised me like his grandson; I've always called him that. Maya, Jacques's wife, painted it."

"She's very talented. This place is so amazing I can't imagine owning it and then not living here. Will your family return soon?"

His family circumstances obviously confused her. Probably more so because Jacques kept a hacker on salary to comb the internet for references to the de Launay family and delete them. To the world, Jacques, Maya, and Grand-Papa had disappeared off the face of the earth for no reason. Love screwed more than drivers' careers.

"Not for a while. They're living elsewhere."

"I'm so sorry for you."

"For me?" He wasn't the one who'd given up everything to keep the woman he loved safe.

"Yes. I know what it's like not to have family to support you. It must be especially difficult in your job. You need someone to share the ups and downs with." She'd taken a couple of steps closer to him. Her hand hovered in the air for a second before dropping to her side. Had she been about to touch him? A quiver raced through him. What the hell? Was he so desperate for a woman that even near contact set him off? Maybe they should go to Paris where the chances of him hooking up were greater. But that thought made his stomach roil.

Oh, for Christ's sake, Daniel. Do not get hung up on the pretty brunette with the chameleon personality.

"I have my team," he replied, trying to shrug off her concern.

He was saved from further psychoanalysis by the arrival of the hot drinks.

"Do you prefer tea or coffee?" he asked. "I guess after two months together I'll know exactly what you want."

Her eyes flared for a moment before she looked away. "Tea would be great, with just a spot of milk," she added as he poured her a cup. "To fast-forward in our get-to-know-each-other quest, I drink coffee in the morning, tea after lunch. And I have one glass of red wine after … after dinner." There it was again, the hesitation, the hint of a secret.

"Good to know." He handed her the cup and gestured for her to take a seat. She settled on the sofa. A gentleman would take the chair opposite so they could converse easily. Instead he sat next to her, so close he could feel the heat off her thigh. The teacup rattled on her saucer.

"Alexandra—"

"Please, call me Lexy. People I don't like call me Alexandra."

"And you like me?"

She tilted her head to one side. "The jury's still out on that one. But in the meantime, I prefer to be called Lexy."

"Well, Lexy." He tried the diminutive, but it lacked the richness of her full name. "We're bound to discover things about each other that the other would rather keep private. I want you to know that I'm very good at keeping secrets. And I've had extensive media training. So I'm not likely to blurt out things about your personal life in public. You can trust me." He stared into her eyes to see the effect his speech had on her.

She gazed back as though she could see through to his soul. "All right." She drew out the reply like she was saying what he expected to hear rather than what she truly meant. "The same goes for me. I won't divulge your secrets either. So you can tell me what you were doing with Jacqueline Lefebre the other night." Offer someone a branch and they hit you over the head with the rest of the tree.

He rose from the sofa so suddenly her tea sloshed over into the saucer. "That isn't my secret to tell. You'll have to ask Jacqueline when you meet her. Now, if you'll excuse me, I have emails to answer. Pull the cord next to the mantel when you're done, and Marie or Bertrand will show you to your room."

But rather than head to the home office, he made his way to the library. It was his hideout, and only Marie knew how many hours he'd spent in there as a child, reading and making imaginary friends. But today even his favorite book, *The Great Gatsby*, couldn't hold his attention. His mind kept drifting to Lexy. She was one hell of a distraction. One he couldn't afford at this point in his life.

Damn woman. Why'd she have to be so … real?

Chapter Three

Good thing I'm not a psychologist yet. With that kind of "open up to me" patter, my patients would mow down new arrivals in their haste to get away.

So far, it was a crap start to their eight weeks together. Daniel clearly had abandonment issues. And she'd just left her three-year-old son in order to gallivant around the globe. There was a huge difference between keeping secrets and accepting them. If Mr. "I don't need anyone" discovered she had a child, his cooperation would cease and she'd be out of a job and risk losing her son altogether.

Except Max had been so excited about an extended sleep-over with Andrew that he'd barely said good-bye to her before bounding back into the blanket fort Sonia had made so the boys could sleep together. It'd broken her heart that Max would rather sleep on the floor than snuggled up in his bed in the corner of her room where she could hear him breathing at night. A soft, gentle sound that had kept her going during her darkest days. Sheesh, now who needed counseling?

Her phone binged with an incoming message.

Sonia: Just wanted to let you know that Max is fine. He says he's going to miss you, but he's going to be very brave and not cry because that would make you sad and he wants you to be happy.

Lexy: Tell him I love him and miss him, too. And it's okay to cry sometimes.

Like I'm perilously close to doing now.

Sonia: No one is going to cry. Have an adventure! You deserve it.

What did they say about the road to hell?

Lexy: I'll try.

Sonia: You HAVE to. I'm now living vicariously through you. Do it for me.

Lexy: Of the two of us, I think you've been having fun more recently than me.

Sonia: Sigh. Baby bellies don't lie. Use protection.

Lexy: This is a business trip.

Sonia: You keep telling yourself that, honey. Maybe one of us will believe it.

Lexy: I'm going now. Chat with you later. And thanks again.

She blinked back the tears. Max would be fine. They'd promised to Skype every night at bedtime. She'd left him with someone who loved him almost as much as she did herself. And the money she was able to pay Sonia would help her family through a tough time. Everyone was happy. So why did she still feel guilty? Ah, the joys of motherhood. No matter how much you tried or did, you always thought you could have done more.

Finishing her tea, she hesitated to pull the cord by the mantel. It seemed such a demanding thing to do, like saying, "Come wait on me now." Although, the way the housekeeper had greeted Daniel, he obviously hadn't abused that privilege. But she would like to freshen up before dinner.

She stuck her head out into the hallway, but all she could see were doors and a huge staircase that led to even more rooms upstairs. It would take her days to find the room set aside for her. Besides, it was probably in the servants' quarters. No help for it; she'd have to ring.

Marie was at her side almost before she'd released the cord. "You wish your chamber now?" the housekeeper asked in halting English.

"Yes, although, if you point me in the right direction, I can probably find it on my own if you're busy," Lexy replied in French.

A huge smile creased the older woman's face. "Not at all, *ma cherie*. You are the first woman Daniel has brought home. I can't have you wandering this big house on your own. Where is that boy? He should be looking after you himself. I shall smack him later, yes?" The housekeeper led her up the stairs and then down a long corridor.

"No. It's fine. We're business acquaintances, not in a relationship. He had some work to do."

"Bah, that boy needs a good woman. It's time he stopped playing and settled down." Marie's gaze raked over Lexy, as if to determine whether she was a good woman or a plaything. Before the housekeeper could make her diagnosis, she opened a door and ushered Lexy through.

"Wow. This room is amazing." It was bigger than her whole flat back in London. A large four-poster bed rested against one wall, draped in heavy silks and velvets. Four ten-foot-high windows flooded the room with light. There were even two sofas and a high-back chair arranged around a large marble fireplace. She could quite happily stay right here for the rest of her time in France, ignore Daniel, wherever he was, and just read.

"I have pressed and put away your things. If you need anything else, text me and I'll bring it to you," Marie said as she handed a card with her mobile number to Lexy. "Dinner is at seven thirty, although the family usually meets for drinks half an hour before in the *petit salon* where you had your tea. I'm sure Daniel will keep up that tradition now that he has someone to share his meals with him."

"Thank you, Marie."

The housekeeper left and Lexy explored the room. A very nice bathroom, complete with a claw-footed tub and glass shower enclosure beckoned her. Even the floor tiles were heated. At the other side of the fireplace, a door led to a walk-in wardrobe, all ten feet of it. Lexy's few dresses were hung next to six enormous garment bags. Max wasn't the only curious Camparelli. With a shaking hand, she unzipped the first one.

A stunning gown in deep chocolate brown shot through with gold thread shimmered in the light. The fabric was so soft it felt like heavy cream. Carefully removing it from the hanger, she held it against her, examining the effect in the full-length mirror at the end of the room. The color emphasized her olive skin tone and even made her drab hair look nice. She rehung the dress and opened the next bag. Another designer gown … this one was peacock blue, with a shockingly short skirt. It would barely cover her backside. A black sheath dress was in the third bag and a red, flowing gown in the fourth. The fifth held an exquisitely cut business suit in a dove-gray color. And the sixth had two jumpsuits, one in an animal print and the other a fluorescent shade of orange. All in her size.

While she was still puzzling over the clothes, there was a knock at her door. It was probably Marie back to give her more information on the dress code for dinner, so Lexy called out, “Come in!”

Would she be expected to wear one of these outfits? She normally ate her dinner in her pajamas with Max snuggled up next to her, smelling all clean, just out of the bath. She blinked back the tears, already missing her little boy, to find Daniel leaning against the door to the wardrobe.

He was so gorgeous she went on the offense to hide her reaction to him. “What are these?”

“Clothes.” His full lips twitched upward, drawing an answering smile from her.

“Thank you for your brilliant insight. Whose clothes?”

“Yours.”

“I didn’t pack these things.”

“Nevertheless, they are yours. If I have to wear Destin Designs in public, then so should you. The helpful receptionist at your company gave me your sizes. There are shoes, too, somewhere.” He stepped into the room and it was as though all the air had been sucked out. He'd had a shower, his hair still slightly damp and curled against the collar of his suit. And God help her, the cologne—it should be illegal for a man to smell that good. She took another deep breath, and his gaze fastened on hers. Busted. "There's also a bottle of perfume for you. It's not bad. Don't you agree?"

"What? Yes, you smell nice. But really, I can't wear these clothes. And I'm not supposed to be seen in public. I'm just to hang around in the background and steer you clear of any mistakes, manage your…"

He put his hand up against the wall behind her, trapping her between the clothes and his tall, hard body. "You think you can manage me?" His minty fresh breath ruffled the wisps of her hair that had sprung free from her bun. She didn't dare lick her lips in case he misinterpreted the action to think she wanted him to kiss her. But man, did she want him to kiss her.

"Not you; your affairs," she said, her voice annoyingly breathless.

He shifted even closer. From this distance she could see his green eyes were flecked with gray. No wonder they were so mesmerizing. "You're planning on pimping me out?" His eyes focused on her lips.

"No, of course not. I'm just here to…" *Why the hell am I here again?* His Adam's apple bobbed as he swallowed, his lips parted slightly, and his eyes softened. He was in full playboy mode, which was pretty powerful stuff to a woman who hadn't had sex since her husband walked out the door almost four years ago. But Lexy wasn't going to fall for that. Still…

He reached past her and fingered the fabric of the

blue dress right next to her ear. "This is my favorite. Will you wear it tonight?"

She had to get control. Now. Before she flung herself at him. Adventure was one thing. Desperation another. "I don't think so. It's not really a dinner-at-home dress."

The back of his fingers brushed her cheek as he withdrew his hand. "Shame. Well, whatever you choose, you'll be beautiful." He took a step back and she drew in a relieved breath, which only filled her head with his scent again and drew his eyes to her breasts. He cleared his throat. "I'll meet you in the *petit salon* at seven. If you lose your way, just shout and I'll organize a search party."

"Yes. Sure. Seven. I'll be there."

With a chuckle, he left. She waited until she heard the bedroom door *click* closed and then flung off her clothes to try on the blue dress. It took a bit of contorting to do the zip up at the back. Obviously it was a gown meant to be done up, or down, by someone else. Probably the reason Daniel liked it. She found the matching shoes in a box on the nearby shelf. Slipping them on, she released her hair from its tight bun and let it fall around her shoulders. She dared one peek at the full-length mirror, then another. The fat girl she'd always be in her mind refused to believe what her eyes were telling her. Holy heck in a teapot she was sexy, if she did say so herself. She almost went in search of Daniel to see if she could knock that self-assured cocky grin off his face.

A few more contortions and a possible dislocated

shoulder later, she managed to undo the zip. She'd save the dress for when she needed a boost to her self-confidence or she was ready to go after her adventure.

***

The *tap-tap* of high heels on the wood floor alerted him to Lexy's arrival. He took a deep breath and then glanced toward the door. She stood in the doorway, wearing the black dress. The fabric hugged her every curve, and although the dress went past her knees the bright red heels she wore drew his eye down the length of her legs. For once her hair was loose, and her curls ran riot around her face. Her beauty was natural, but surprisingly she seemed unaware of how enticing she appeared. More of his blood shifted south and he moved to the bar, hidden in a piece of antique furniture, to disguise his discomfort.

"Would you like an aperitif? Perhaps a Campari, given your Italian heritage?" he asked.

"Just a glass of wine will do—red, if you have it."

"We're on a winery. Pretty sure we have red wine." He poured the drink then handed her the glass, their fingers grazing as he did so. Her eyes widened and she stared up at him, her lips slightly parted. As in the wardrobe, he forced himself to move away before he kissed her. This intense attraction was damn annoying.

She opened and closed her mouth several times, took a sip of the wine, and finally asked, "So, what made you want to become a Formula 1 driver?"

At last a topic he could talk on endlessly. "When I

was ten years old, my grandfather took me to a race at Magny-Cours, and I fell in love with the sport. It's all I've wanted to do ever since."

"I wanted to be a driver once. But my father told me girls can't drive and I'd be better off following my mother into modeling."

"Your father's an ass, but I guess you already know that. Had you fought for your dream, you could have been the first woman driver. Your father had the clout to make it happen."

She shrugged. "I never wanted it badly enough; it was just a passing fancy. And shortly after that my parents split up, so I didn't stick around F1. Plus, want to know something funny?"

"Sure." She'd relaxed enough to settle on the sofa, her dark hair spilling over the back of the cream upholstery. For a second he imagined it spread across his pillow, or better yet, his chest. He sat in the chair opposite so he could watch her face as she revealed her first secret.

"I've never even learned to drive."

He put his glass down. "We could fix that. Driving's easy. I'll teach you."

"Really?" She leaned forward, her hair caressing her face now lit with delight.

"Of course. We have four days, twelve cars in the garage, and several kilometers of private roads on the estate. It'll be fun."

"'It'll be fun.' Those sound like famous last words. Are you sure you don't want to add, 'what could go wrong?' Like me crashing and you getting seriously injured and unable to drive for the rest of the season?"

"I'll wear my crash helmet. And we'll start by driving my brother's Land Rover. You could roll that baby several times with no ill effects."

"Your brother may have something to say about that."

"I won't tell him if you won't. Come on, don't tell me you're scared."

"Of course I'm not scared, I'm just…"

"Running out of excuses?"

She laughed. "Yeah, something like that. All right. But if I'm really awful then we'll give up and never speak of it again."

"I never give up. Not when it's something I want."

Her eyes narrowed. "Are we still talking about me learning to drive?"

Time for a gear change. "How did you end up in advertising?" He'd met a lot of people in that line of work, and she didn't fit the mold.

She bit down on the side of her finger, then, seeming to realize what she was doing, sat on her hand. "I kind of ended up there. I'm working on a psychology degree. Believe it or not, the two fields are related."

"And that's what you really want to do, be a psychologist?"

"Originally I wanted to be a neuroscientist and study addiction, but even becoming a psychologist seems a distant dream these days."

She was back to chewing on her finger. If they weren't going to spend the next two months discussing the weather, he'd better find something they had in common. Maybe her connection with Formula 1. "You know we're likely to run into your father at some point in the next two months. He still attends most of the races."

"I know. But I doubt he'll even recognize me."

Dieu, this woman was a conversation minefield. He thought *his* family was screwed up. At least his mother contacted him every so often to try to get money out of him.

"When was the last time you saw him?"

"On my sixteenth birthday. The visit didn't end well and he never came back."

"Must have been some argument."

"It was."

"How old were you when your parents split?"

"Seven. But I don't remember them ever being happy. They always argued. My mother told me she deliberately got pregnant so my father would marry her. When they divorced I lost more than my dad … I lost my whole family. I was born into F1. All the drivers and their wives and crews were like my uncles and aunts. I thought every child spoke several languages. Once I started school, though, my mother wanted me to have more stability. So she settled in the UK where she was from, as she'd never become very proficient in Italian. We still went to a few races a year, but it wasn't the same and the arguing was even worse. One year my mother decided to surprise my father by showing up unexpectedly. She pulled me out of school and we flew to Rio… And walked in on my father having sex with some woman."

"*Mon Dieu*, I'm sorry."

She shrugged. "I don't think it was the first time he'd cheated. But she'd had enough. They divorced. I stayed with my mother. My father made a token effort to stay in touch for the first few years. Now he only contacts me when he's getting married again and tries to pretend I'm still part of his life." She let out a harsh laugh. "Some people get Christmas cards. I get wedding invitations."

"Maybe this will give you two a chance to reconnect."

A weary sigh escaped her perfect lips. "Too much time has passed. Too much anger. After the divorce my mother really poisoned my mind against him, and for a long time I hated him, too. But now that I'm an adult I can see there are two sides to every story. My mother was very shallow and self-centered and hard to live with. But I still can't forgive him for cheating on Mum. If he wanted to end things, he should have done it the honorable way."

"Is there an honorable way to end a marriage?"

"I don't know. At least wait until the divorce papers are signed to start banging someone else."

There was a world of bitterness in her tone. Did she have personal experience aside from that of her parents?

"Are you divorced?"

She looked away before replying. "Yes. And to answer your next question, no, I wasn't unfaithful." She took in a shuddering breath. "What about your parents? I take it your mother is still alive, albeit unwelcome."

"*Maman* tried the great con and got caught. She was married to Jacques's father but having affairs on the side. Except she screwed up and got pregnant. Thought she could pass me off as her husband's child, but unknown to her he'd had a vasectomy so he wouldn't get any of his lovers pregnant. They separated, but when Jacques's father died his grandfather asked if I could come live with them so Jacques wasn't lonely."

"Why didn't your mother just take the two of you? You're both her sons, aren't you?" She obviously hadn't met his mother.

"Oh, no, she was more than happy to get rid of me. I cramped her lifestyle."

"What about your father?"

"I've no idea who he is. Clearly someone who went around knocking up women on the weekend." Not a person Daniel was interested in meeting, dying or not.

"That's a bit harsh for someone with your reputation."

"And I'd have thought a woman in your line of work would know better than to believe everything the media spews out. Especially when you've capitalized on that particular aspect of my life."

She blinked, and, unless he was imagining it, her features softened. "You're right. I'm sorry; I shouldn't have said that."

Their gazes locked in a silent battle, each trying to see beyond the other's mask. Bertrand stood in the doorway and cleared his throat before speaking. "Dinner is ready when you are."

Daniel rose, took her now-empty wine glass, and placed it on the tray. They walked side by side to the dining room. The wall was back between them. The delicious meal his chef had prepared would taste like cardboard if he didn't do something. "What do you usually do after dinner?" he asked.

"I'm pretty boring. If I don't have work to do, I read. Books are my addiction."

Finally, something they had in common. "In that case, I have a surprise for you."

"A good surprise?" Her eyebrows were raised, widening her chocolate pudding eyes.

Warmth rushed through him. "The best."

Chapter Four

Dinner went better than he'd hoped. He'd taken to eating in the kitchen with the staff since Jacques and Grand-Papa had left. He'd missed the ritual of getting dressed up and eating in the formal dining room—a room that held so many happy memories for him of catching up with his family at the end of a busy day.

When not berating him for something she knew nothing about, Lexy was interesting and funny and unassuming—a refreshing change from the women he normally dined with. If they could maintain this détente, the next two months might not be too bad.

She understood his world and could talk intelligently on a number of subjects, including the recent engine changes and the aerodynamic adjustments required to cope with the increase in horsepower. But when it came to discussing her own life and areas of interest, Lexy was surprisingly quiet. She hadn't been to see any films in the past two years, and her last holiday had been to visit her mother. She'd led a life so far removed from the F1 world—how would she cope with the constant travel, media scrutiny, and endless rounds of parties and events at which he was expected to appear?

She finished her second glass of wine, which she'd nursed all through dinner, declining when he offered to top it up.

"I ate all my vegetables. Do I get my surprise now?" Lexy asked, a mischievous smile playing about her lips. There was something infectious about her lack of artifice. He was so used to plastic women who only wanted to be with him to claim some sort of prize in a celebrity scavenger hunt. They didn't really want *him*; just to bed a driver.

"Of course. Although I probably would have shown you even if you hadn't eaten your vegetables." He rose from his chair and waited for her at the end of the table.

"You're going to be an indulgent father, aren't you?"

"I don't plan to have children. Drivers with families lose their edge. I won't risk that. Plus, as you can testify, the F1 circuit isn't the greatest place to bring up little ones."

A shadow crossed her eyes; someday he'd learn to think faster before he spoke. There was a limit to the number of times someone wanted to remember their turbulent past in one day.

"Are you planning on staying in Formula 1 when you're finished driving?" she asked.

"I haven't really given it much thought. I've still got at least ten years as a driver; I guess I'll figure it out when I get closer to retirement." He paused outside the door to the library. Would she be disappointed? Think this was a lame surprise?

"This isn't your bedroom, is it?" She eyed him warily but didn't step away. Was she game? Standing close, her intoxicating scent drifting over him, lust was reasserting itself.

"No. Although, if you prefer…" He inched closer to her, but still she didn't back down. He could read the war going on in her. She was interested but not sure it was a good idea. That made two of them.

He flung open the door and waited for her to step into the room. It featured floor-to-ceiling bookshelves, and Daniel had convinced Jacques to have special airflow units installed to keep the books in the best condition possible. Some of them dated back to the eighteenth century. Those precious editions were housed behind glass at the back of the library.

"Oh. My. God. This is spectacular." Her eyes darted from shelf to shelf like a child in a candy store. It was exactly the response he'd hoped for.

"When I was eight, I set the goal of reading every single book in this room."

"How's that going?" She reached a hand out to touch a book but drew it back before she made contact.

He pulled his favorite book off a shelf, a first edition of *The Great Gatsby*. "Not so well. I'm away too much. Plus I keep getting drawn back to my favorites." Handing her the book, he strolled over to the next bookshelf. He had other fantasies centered in this room, ones developed after he'd hit puberty. Also as yet unfulfilled.

"Which are your favorites?"

He took her hand and led her over to the bookshelf next to the mantel. The original wood-burning fireplace had been exchanged for a gas one, and covered in glass to protect the books. Across from the fire he'd moved in an overstuffed, navy-blue sofa. More than one night he'd slept there, his book falling from his fingers onto the Persian carpet.

He pointed at the ladder that slid on a metal bar around the room. "The third shelf from the top. Aside from Gatsby, I love the writings of Zola, Dumas, de Balzac, and Hugo. Many are first editions. Would you like to see?"

"May I?" The reverence in her tone set off a flutter in his belly.

"The thing with books is, if you don't touch them and love them, they're just a bunch of papers stuck together."

He couldn't resist going up behind her on the ladder. After all, he wouldn't want her to fall and injure herself. *Yeah, right.* When she attained the height of the shelf in question, he reached around her and pulled out a copy of *The Three Musketeers*. "I was gutted when Grand-Papa told me there were no more musketeers. Good thing he took me to my first F1 race, or I'd have been an unemployed swordsman, looking for a fight."

She chuckled and her delectable ass wriggled against his abdomen. The fluttery feeling in his stomach moved south, raising other desires. He inhaled deeply of her scent, and clutched the ladder so he didn't fall. *Dieu*, she smelled good. Subtle flowers with a hint of heat. Was that what she was under all that reserve? A passionate tigress just waiting to be released? Now, wasn't that a mental picture to keep a man from sleeping. Or concentrating when he needed to.

"Good thing you didn't read *Dr. Jekyll & Mr. Hyde*," she said, her voice breathless.

He slipped on his playboy smile. "Have you read *Madame Bovary*? This copy is in French, but I think there's an English one around here somewhere." His hand brushed against the side of her breast as he reached to the shelf once more.

"I've read it. In French." She shifted against him again and he nearly lost his grip.

Falling and breaking his arm was not how he wanted to end his race season. He retreated down the ladder; as she descended after him, his gaze fixed on her ass. It was so perfect he clenched his hands into fists to stop from reaching out.

When she was finally back on the floor, she turned to him and shook her head. "I can't get over the fact that the playboy racer loves to read."

Should he tell her? No, he needed the illusion for protection. It kept good women, like Lexy seemed to be, from getting too close. Bimbos who liked his man-whore reputation were no risk to his career.

"I have to have something to do while recovering from all the women I sleep with."

Her eyes searched his and the lie burned in his throat. He looked away before she could discover the truth.

"I don't believe you," she eventually said.

"About reading or sleeping with lots of women?"

"I'm not sure. One is a lie. I can see it in your eyes. You're conflicted about something. And the man standing in front of me isn't the same one I just had dinner with. Which is the real you, Daniel?"

"As you don't believe my words, maybe this will answer your question." His arm snaked around her waist and pulled her body up to his. Her voluptuous breasts pressed against his chest, causing him to drag in a ragged breath. His other hand tilted her chin up before sliding into her hair. Her mouth opened; whether to protest or welcome he wasn't sure. Either way he took advantage, as a playboy would, and kissed her.

She tasted of the rich chocolate pudding they'd had for dessert and the red wine she'd sipped throughout dinner. Her lips were soft, full, and completely devoid of all the fillers and injections that made some women's lips like kissing a bike tire. She was naturally, one-hundred-percent sexy.

The kiss went on. If he tried to retreat, she'd press forward, and vice versa. Their hands explored, flitting all too briefly over areas that deserved to be savored. When his head swam because he forgot to breathe, he pulled back. Her face was flushed, her chest rose and fell rapidly, and the soft, dreamy look in her eyes almost made him go back for seconds. But he was already in danger of drowning in desire for her. If he wanted to make it through the next eight weeks and claim the championship, he had to keep his focus on driving and off the delectable woman in his arms.

He released his hold and stepped back. He had to clear his throat twice before he could speak. "Have I answered your question?" He had kissed her to make a point, hadn't he?

She ran a shaking hand through her hair. "Do you

never take a break from trying to get a woman in bed with you?"

"Isn't that why you're here? To make sure I sleep with a different woman every night, as long as they're not married?"

"Well, I'm not a candidate for *femme du jour*. Don't count on me to fill your quota."

"Just when I think your opinion of me can't get any lower, it drops another meter. This is going to be a long eight weeks."

Before she could respond, he left the room. He should be happy she believed his playboy persona.

He wasn't.

***

Lexy pulled her hair back into a severe bun, hoping it would make her look professional, calm, and collected. None of the things she was feeling. After *the kiss*, and then once again insulting Daniel, she'd tossed and turned for hours in her bed. When had she become such a bitch?

If she were truly honest with herself—which was never comfortable—she'd kissed him as much as he'd kissed her. There'd been no coercion or seduction; it'd been mutual passion. Damn, it was a fabulous kiss. Apparently she had no control when it came to Daniel, and would have to resist lip-locks with him in the future.

Why resist? the devil on her shoulder asked.

Because she was a flipping single mum with a son

to care for. She couldn't throw away her career and Max's future on an affair with a racecar driver.

But he's discreet. No one need ever know, the devil added. *And didn't Sonia tell you to have some fun for once*?

This might be her only chance for a casual fling in the next fifteen years before Max went to university. Hells bells, what a depressing thought. Another fifteen years without sex. Although until that kiss with Daniel, it hadn't been anything she'd missed all that much. But maybe that had more to do with her ex than her lack of libido. Because it had taken ten minutes in a cold shower to even return her body temperature to something resembling normal last night.

She pasted on a pleasant smile, the one she reserved for the neighbor who always complained that Max was too loud in the morning. The dining room was empty, however. No Daniel in sight. Shouldn't she feel relieved?

Marie appeared. "Daniel has already eaten. He's in the gym doing his exercises. What can I get you for breakfast?"

Lexy eyed the basket of pastries on the sideboard and her mouth watered. It seemed temptation was going to be the word of the day. Next to the pastries sat a bowl filled with yogurt cups. Well, she needed to practice restraint somewhere. "I'll just have a yogurt and a coffee," she said, moving toward the table.

"Bah, you young women these days are too skinny," Marie replied.

Lexy could kiss her for the compliment. If Marie

knew the issues Lexy'd had with her weight, she'd understand. But she didn't want to seem ungracious. "Dinner last night was so delicious, I'm still full. But I promise to eat more at lunch."

She'd just finished her breakfast when Daniel strolled into the room. His dark hair was disheveled, his face flushed from his exercise. He had a towel slung around his shoulders and his t-shirt clung to his muscled torso. She refused to allow her eyes to venture farther south.

"Good morning, Lexy. Did you sleep well?"

Her gaze fixated on his lips, remembering their mastery last night. "Perfectly." Her breathless voice gave her away.

"Liar. You tossed and turned like I did."

"I … I was upset at being rude to you once again. I'm sorry. I shouldn't have said what I did. As long as you abide by the behavior clause in your contract, I'll keep my mouth shut in future."

A knowing smile curved his lips. "How very professional of you."

Yes, that's what she was, professional. Not frustrated at all. "Are you still willing to teach me to drive?"

"Absolutely. I'll just grab a shower and bring the Land Rover around to the front of the house. Meet you there in twenty minutes? Unless, of course, this whole professional thing is just a mask and you'd rather join me in the shower?"

She swallowed. "Front of the house, twenty minutes."

The vehicle waiting for her at the designated time was massive. Did he really think she could drive that?

Daniel hopped out, his jeans clinging to his thighs, the top three buttons of his shirt undone, his sleeves rolled up. Her mouth went dry, whether from fear of what she was about to do or his incredible sexiness, she didn't want to analyze.

Coward.

She climbed up into the driver's seat, which was on the wrong side. It should have made her feel more comfortable, sitting in what would be the passenger side of the vehicle on a British car. Except the steering wheel and pedals before her negated that idea. But if she did manage to move out of London with Max, she'd need to be able to drive. And who better to teach her than a professional driver?

"First, you have to move the seat so you're comfortable." Daniel took her hand and showed her where the buttons were to reposition the seat. He then helped her adjust the mirrors.

"It's so big. Don't you have anything smaller?"

"I've never had a woman complain about the size before," he said, waggling his eyebrows. She leveled her best "I am not amused" stare at him. "It's the only one we have with an automatic transmission," he continued. "I thought you'd prefer to master steering and braking before we move on to gear changes."

"Right." She glanced over at him once more. "Are you sure I can do this?"

"Absolutely. If you can stop yourself from punching your annoying boss in the face, then you have the ability to handle this."

Maybe instead of learning to drive she should channel that control into forgetting Daniel's kiss. "Here goes nothing." She put the car in drive and pressed down on the accelerator. The SUV lurched forward like it was shot from a cannon. Quickly she stomped on the brake, sending Daniel flying into the dashboard.

He put on his seat belt then said, "Well, you've got the F1 start down. Let's try again with a little less enthusiasm."

This time she pressed more gently and the vehicle crept forward. After two laps around the fountain in the circular driveway, Daniel pointed toward the back of the house. "I think you've got the hang of it now. Let's go for a drive."

"What? Outside? I'm not licensed."

"Don't worry. We'll stay on private roads."

He directed her down a narrow path with hedges on both sides that reminded her of the country lane to her mother's cottage. Except at the end of this drive she wouldn't have to cope with a depressed, morbidly obese former model who'd pulled her daughter down into the abyss with her.

"Relax," Daniel said, running his finger along the white of her knuckles. "You're doing excellent."

She willed her muscles to release, but she was too tense, too aware of the man next to her. They stopped after a few minutes while Daniel opened a gate in the ten-foot-high stone wall. While he was out of the vehicle, she peeled her hands off the steering wheel and flexed them. This was why people should learn to drive in their teens, when they thought they could do anything. Except teenage Lexy had been so overweight she'd have hardly fit behind the wheel.

Eventually they arrived at a small lake and Daniel told her to put the vehicle in park and turn off the engine. Stiffly, she got out to join him by the shore. In the distance, the chateau stood tall and proud, a testament to his family's wealth. Except she knew how empty and lonely the house now was. Appearances were deceptive. And not only with buildings.

"You come here often?" she asked when Daniel's silence became uncomfortable.

"Every time I'm home."

"It's beautiful; I can see why it's a favorite place."

"I spent a lot of time here as a teen; when I wasn't racing, that is." His green eyes stared into hers. "I was reading, not making out with girls."

"I didn't say anything," she protested. Sure, she'd thought it, but he couldn't read minds.

He ran a hand through his hair and then turned back towards the lake. "Lexy, I'm not going to apologize for last night. I didn't kiss you because I hadn't met my quota of women for the week. I've wanted to kiss you since you walked into that *maudit* boardroom in London, looking like the sexiest librarian I've ever imagined. But I get it that you don't feel the same. So, from now on I'm hands off; not because I don't want you, but because I respect you."

"What if I don't want to be hands off?"

When he looked at her again his eyes smoldered and his sexy smile was back. "Then you have to make the first move."

She broke the eye contact this time. Damn, it was hard to resist him when he was all sensitive and caring. She almost wished he'd revert to the playboy so she could shut him down. Battling her desires was no fun at all.

Hadn't she learned her lesson from Wesley? Her ex had been all sweetness and light until they were married. Once his ring was on her finger, he'd turned into a dictator and treated her like a servant.

Yet despite all the nasty things she'd said to Daniel, he hadn't once retaliated. It was going to take more than her halfway-to-a-psychology-degree experience to figure him out.

If she discovered what made him tick, would it then blow up in her face? The last thing she needed was to make the same mistake twice. Especially when there were so many great new ones to make.

Chapter Five

Lexy pulled the straightener through her hair, trying to tame the frizz. It had been years since she'd bothered to flatten it, and it was taking twice as long as she remembered. She glanced at the clock—in ten minutes she was supposed to meet Daniel in the *petit salon.* And she still hadn't decided what to wear. Which Daniel would show up at dinner tonight? Playboy Daniel with his slick moves and devastating smile, or the more insidious and harder-to-resist gentleman Daniel—the one who held her hand at the lake when she'd slipped going back to the vehicle and who was more excited to show her his books than his supercar collection?

The drive home from the lake had taken half the time, as she'd acquired a little confidence. Daniel had trusted her to drive into the underground garage. Given the other vehicles parked there, she'd been glad he'd selected the Land Rover for her to practice with. Every other car probably cost more than her flat. Max, who seemed to have genetically inherited a love of fast cars from his grandfather, would have shrieked with joy at so many of his favorites in one place.

Daniel had been a bit quieter on the drive back but praised her again when she got them home without crashing. A man who routinely drove more than 200 miles an hour, he hadn't complained once at her snail's pace.

Her hair was as good as it was going to get, so she crossed to the wardrobe and did eeny meeny miney moe, Max's favorite selection algorithm, to pick her outfit. The red dress won and she slipped it on with a wicked pair of black stilettos. If heaven were a shoe collection, she was dancing on the clouds already. They were way beyond her budget, so she was going to wear them every chance she got. Which would she miss more when these eight weeks were over: Daniel or the shoes?

When she entered the *petit salon* she had her answer. Daniel. There were just some things a man could do for a girl that even the most amazing shoes couldn't. He was so stunningly gorgeous, wearing a dark suit, crisp white shirt, and burgundy tie that her breath whooshed out. He turned, his green eyes appraising her, and from the slow, sensuous smile that curved his lips, he appreciated what he saw. This was new for her, feeling desirable. She liked it. It was as if her internal lamp had finally been plugged into an electrical outlet.

Like the previous night, dinner flew by in a blur as they discussed the upcoming races and what she knew of the tracks. She asked after some of the people she remembered from her childhood who still hung around F1. Every time Daniel tried to steer the conversation to her current life, she maneuvered it back to his career. After all, his was the glamorous lifestyle. Her working, cleaning, and worrying she wasn't doing enough for Max would hardly keep an adrenaline-junkie like

Daniel interested five minutes.

She drank almost the whole bottle of wine by herself, maybe a bit too much. Daniel rarely touched his glass. Not surprising; his job required complete control.

Usually she was more restrained. Being solely responsible for Max meant she'd had to play it safe for so long. Just for once she wanted to let loose and enjoy herself. And wasn't she in the perfect position to do that now? Eight weeks with the sexiest man alive, who had said he wanted her. What was she waiting for?

Plus, wouldn't it be better to throw herself at Daniel now, where they didn't have an audience if, once he discovered what was hidden under her clothes, he decided he wasn't interested in her after all? Wesley had been so disgusted by her body he'd only have sex with her with the lights off. While the logical side of her brain said she couldn't paint every man with her ex's brush, she also couldn't forget three hellish months of marriage. This time with Daniel would be just an affair. No heartbreak waited for her at the end. She'd call the shots. She'd be the one to walk away this time. Then she could go back to being good-girl, single mum Lexy, but this time with a secret smile.

"Want to go to the library? I could show you some of the old books at the back," Daniel suggested as she placed her serviette on the table beside her. She searched his face but couldn't find a hint of the playboy. He'd been a perfect gentleman all evening, apart from the lustful look he'd given her when she'd first arrived in the *petit salon*. Would he really wait for her to make the first move?

"I'll meet you there in ten minutes," she replied, forcing an enigmatic smile onto her face. Maybe he'd think she was going to "slip into something more comfortable." In reality, she had to call Max before he went to bed, because as much as she wanted to start her adventure she was still first and foremost a mum.

Except Max was already asleep when she called. With Sonia's husband out of work, he'd taken the boys to the park to play football so Sonia could rest. Max and Andrew had been so tired they'd barely made it through dinner and a bath before conking out. Lexy hid her disappointment behind a smile and promised to call first thing in the morning.

When she stepped into the library, soft music was playing, the gas fireplace was on, and Daniel lounged on the chair. He'd removed his jacket and tie and undone a couple of buttons on his shirt. She swallowed, her mouth suddenly dry, her hand shaking as she tucked a strand of hair behind her ear. He'd laid the groundwork for a seduction, but she had to take it from there.

And if they were going to get physical, she'd have to tell him about her body.

"That was quick," Daniel commented as she perched on the edge of the sofa.

She put her phone down on the side table. "The person I wanted to speak with wasn't available. I'll try again tomorrow morning."

He nodded and stared into the fire for a moment. "Would you like to see the books?"

Damn, it hadn't been a line; he really meant to show her his literary collection.

"Sure." She accompanied him to the back of the room. Leaning against the wall was a painted portrait of Daniel in his racing gear. Except his face was blurry. "Is this another of your sister-in-law's paintings? I guess she didn't have time to finish it before she left." Lexy moved closer, drawn by the image as much as by the man.

"It's done. Maya said that when I'm in my racing gear I know exactly who I am. But when I'm away from the track, I'm not so sure." There was a challenge in his voice.

"Well, that's not uncommon. Your entire focus is on driving. To be the best in your sport, you have to be single-minded."

"Why do I sense there's a 'but' in there somewhere?" He crossed his arms over his abdomen. Did he realize he was mirroring the stance in the photo?

"It's not healthy. Not in the long run. You need something outside of F1, away from the track, to make you happy. If something were to happen, if you weren't able to drive any more, what would you do?"

"I don't know. Hang around here and actually read all these books?" He tried to laugh it off, but she'd seen the consequences of not having anything in life to keep a person from spiraling into depression.

This was her chance. "Let me tell you a story. But you'll need a drink for this one." Actually she needed the drink but didn't want to imbibe alone. By telling him a bit more about her past, she'd be able to discern if he'd be turned off by her body or not. With one last glance at the portrait, she returned to the fireplace.

"Sounds serious." He walked over to a cabinet and returned a minute later with two glasses of amber liquid. Expecting whiskey, she was surprised at the sweet smell. "Cognac," he explained. "Not really my thing, but my brother likes it."

She took a tentative sip, enjoying the way it rolled on her tongue, making her mouth a little numb before she swallowed. She sank down onto the sofa, relieved when he sat next to her. He fiddled with the material of her dress, sliding the fabric between his long fingers. Her body tingled, waiting for his touch. Maybe she should just skip the story and kiss him.

"I told you a bit about my parents. What I didn't tell you was that my mother had a complete breakdown after the divorce. She was a model when she met my father. Not a huge success but pretty enough—tall and elegant with long, blond hair. I'm sure you know the type."

He nodded, his eyes roaming her face. If he was looking for some resemblance to her mother, he wouldn't find it. Unfortunately, she'd inherited more of her father's genes.

"All she had were her looks and her marriage, which was really her ticket to an easy life. Papa had money. She liked money. When she caught my father cheating, she figured her looks weren't enough anymore to keep a man, so she let herself go. Actually, letting herself go is a misnomer; it was more like she threw herself off a cliff."

"But she had you."

"I wasn't enough either. My mother was very narcissistic. She never really understood my father and the pressure he was under, and I don't think she ever tried. It was all about the glamour and the parties for her. Anyway, after it was over, she sank into a deep depression and dragged me down with her. She ate constantly and insisted that I join her. Remember I said my father last saw me on my sixteenth birthday? Well, what he saw was a morbidly obese teenager who could barely get off the sofa to greet him."

She searched Daniel's face, expecting to see disgust. She saw compassion instead. He put his drink down and took her hand in his, rubbing his thumb across her knuckles. "No one looking at you now would ever think you were once overweight."

"Thanks. But I know I'm still a little heavy. Certainly I'm not like the majority of women you come across on the circuit." Within a week she'd be standing next to some of them. It was going to be obvious.

"Can I tell you something the majority of women don't seem to realize? Most men prefer women with substance. When I'm with a skinny woman, I worry that if I hold her too tight, she'll snap and I'll be left holding the pieces." He raised his arms as though dangling two sections of woman. "Excuse me, I seem to have broken this one. Terribly sorry."

She smiled at his attempt to humor her.

He drew a circle on the back of her hand with his index finger, and she repressed the shiver of delight. "When did you lose the excess weight?"

Finishing her drink, she put the glass down on the table next to Daniel's. "As soon as I went away to college and was away from my mother, I could make my own eating choices and I became healthier. I started to exercise and gradually got slimmer. But my body still carries the evidence. I have masses of stretch marks, and although I've had one excess skin removal surgery, I've lost more weight since and have saggy bits. My skin's a bit crepey…"

She checked again for revulsion on his face but saw none. Instead he stood and began unbuttoning his shirt. Okay, not the reaction she was expecting, but she was fine with it. More than fine. He tossed his shirt onto the sofa and pointed at a long, jagged scar near his shoulder. The firelight danced on his skin, and her fingers itched to join the party.

"I smashed my clavicle in a racing accident when I was fifteen. The bone came right through the skin. And here"—he took her hand and ran her fingers over a bump on his side—"I broke a rib luging down the stairs on the cook's baking sheets when I was seven. I never told Grand-Papa I was injured, so it healed with a bump. I have others."

She wasn't quite sure what his point was; she was too mesmerized by the feel of his warm skin under her fingers. He took her hand in his again and pulled her to her feet and into his arms, his eyes searching hers as she raised her face. "What I'm trying to say"—his voice was deep and husky—"is that my scars are due to accidents and stupidity. Any marks you bear are battle scars acquired in your war against obesity, your fight to save your life. You shouldn't be ashamed. Wear them with pride. It takes a strong woman to pull herself out of the abyss."

She blinked back the tears forming in her eyes. Not even her husband who had claimed to love her had made her feel good about her body.

"Thank you," she managed past the lump in her throat.

His hand cupped her cheek, his thumb rubbing over her bottom lip, pulling it gently away from her teeth. She leaned in closer, the heat from his naked chest encouraging her to snuggle. "Lexy, I said I'd wait for you to make the first move."

"Consider me moved."

"Are you sure? If you need more time—"

"No." He dropped his hand and she quickly wrapped hers around his waist, drawing him back to her. "I mean no, I don't need more time. But I should tell you, I'm not very good at sex so don't expect too much."

"Not very good? How is that even possible?"

"My ex-husband—"

"Forget him. This is between you and me. No one else."

He lowered his head and took her lips in a kiss so gentle, so sweet, it shook her to her core. She'd expected raw passion, maybe a bit of frenzied pulling-off of clothes. And despite Sonia's warning, she hadn't come prepared. Hopefully Daniel carried condoms. After all, he was the playboy.

"Dance with me," he whispered against her ear. Ed

Sheeran's "Thinking Out Loud" began to play through the music system. Daniel swayed against her, and her body responded.

"I thought we were going to…"

"In time. We have all night. I want to make this memorable."

All night? In ten minutes he'd be mopping her up off the floor. And as for memorable, seeing as she hadn't had sex in almost four years, she was pretty sure she wouldn't forget this.

***

Daniel moved Lexy's hand from his back and placed it behind his neck. After a moment she threaded her fingers in his hair, her head tucked under his chin. If it weren't for his rock-hard erection, he could stay like this for hours; holding her close, feeling her heartbeat. But she was so tense she needed to relax a lot more before he could take things further.

"Dancing isn't one of my better talents," she mumbled against his neck. Her breath on his overheated skin notched up his internal temperature another couple of digits.

"Let your body move with mine. Follow my lead."

She raised her head and stared at him, a sensuous smile curving her lips. "I'll follow your lead. For now."

"That's it, *ma cherie*. Show me the fire." Although if she got any hotter, he'd need his flame-resistant overalls. *Dieu*, she was sexy. Her ex must've been a real ass.

He stroked a hand down her back as they swayed to the music. With a swift move, he swiveled her around so her back was to his chest, both her hands behind his neck. He dropped kisses down her throat as he caressed her sides, lingering for a fraction of a second on her breasts before continuing downward. He feathered touches over her lower stomach before settling on her hips. Pressing himself into her, he let her feel his hardness. She wriggled against him, and he bit back a groan.

"Don't ever let anyone tell you you're not sexy," he said. "Every time I see you I want to take you in my arms and feel you like this." His hands made the journey in reverse, lingering longer on her breasts. His thumbs flickered over her nipples, which hardened through the layers of fabric. Lexy was breathing rapidly, a low moan of pleasure escaping her lips as he touched her abdomen again.

"Daniel." She breathed his name and a shot of pure lust arrowed through him.

Another song came on, this one with a faster tempo, but he kept their rhythm to the same languid pace. He really should update his seduction playlist. They swayed together as he explored her body with his hands, tasting her skin with his lips and tongue. Desperate for more flesh-to-flesh contact, he worked the fabric of her dress up until he could slide his hand underneath and feel the soft skin of her thigh. She was quivering with each touch, her breath coming in pants. Her hands were still locked behind his head, holding tightly, as though she were afraid that if she let go she'd fall.

He turned her again so he could work the zipper at the back of her dress. When it was undone he put both hands on her face and kissed her deeply. It had to be her choice to remove her clothes. As their tongues dueled he felt the fabric fall to her feet.

Releasing her lips, he stepped back a bit, holding both her hands in his so she couldn't cover herself. "You are exquisite," he said.

She looked about to argue so he kissed her again, leading her hands to the buckle at his waist. Her fingers grazed his hardness as she undid the belt and then the zipper on his fly. It was his turn to moan. He trailed kisses down her neck; her quiver echoed through him. *Dieu*, she was so responsive.

Trying to maintain any semblance of dancing was no longer feasible. He removed the rest of his clothes, hoping Lexy would do the same. She stood between him and the fire still wearing her bra and panties, the dim light preventing him from truly appreciating her body. But what he did see was fantastic.

"I can't believe I'm doing this," she whispered.

"Are you having second thoughts?"

"No. It's just, you're Daniel Michaud, world-famous racecar driver, possibly the sexiest man alive…"

"Possibly?" He quirked an eyebrow. *Maudit*, not her, too. Another woman who wanted the driver, not the man.

"Definitely the sexiest man alive. I'm just … well, me, a girl who's only ever had sex with one man."

"Lexy…"

"Just promise me one thing."

"What's that?"

"If this goes horribly wrong, we pretend it never happened and return to being friends."

"Horribly wrong? What kind of sex have you had?"

"Obviously not the good kind."

"Are we going to see if this is the good kind, or do you want to talk both of us out of this?"

She unfastened her bra and let it drop to the floor then threaded her fingers into his hair and pulled his head down towards hers. As their lips were about to touch, she suddenly jerked her head to one side. An oddly familiar tune filled the air. That children's song was definitely not on his playlist.

"I have to get that," she said. Releasing him, she grabbed his shirt off the sofa and tugged it on before picking up her phone.

"Hello?" A hint of panic tinged Lexy's question.

"Mummy!" a young boy's excited voice echoed through the room.

Mummy? Ice replaced the heat in his veins. Lexy had a kid?

Chapter Six

Lexy's heart pounded and she pulled Daniel's shirt tighter around her, trying to pretend she hadn't been moments from possibly the greatest night of her life. She forced her eyes to concentrate on her son, checking for signs of illness, and not her disheveled, dazed picture in the corner of the screen.

"Mummy, you look funny," Max said.

"I, uh, I was just getting ready for bed." More likely the sofa, or maybe the floor, or up against a bookshelf… The blood that had drained from her face when she heard Sonia's ringtone now rushed back.

"We didn't say goodnight." Max's sweet voice brought her back from contemplating possible sexual positions.

"I know, darling. I called, but you were already asleep. Are you having fun? Have you been a good boy for Sonia and Mark?" It was damned hard to keep her mind on her son's situation when behind her she could hear Daniel pulling on his trousers. She was careful to keep the phone's camera on her face so Max couldn't see what he'd interrupted. Although, he was probably too young to understand the implication of his mother looking a mess with a naked man in the background.

"I'm being good. But I miss you. When are you coming home?"

"Not for a long while, yet, sweets. Remember, we talked about this. Mummy has to take a long trip for work, but when I get back we're going to have a holiday together."

"Can we go to Disneyland? I saw on the telly, that's where Lighting Queen and Mater live."

"I'm not sure. Disneyland's a long way away. We'll discuss it when I get back. I love you oodles and oodles, Max. Sleep tight and we can chat longer tomorrow." Out of the corner of her eye she could see Daniel with his arms crossed over his bare chest, taking in every nuance of her conversation.

"I love you, too, Mummy. Sonia wants to say 'night as well." He made a kissing face then handed the phone to her friend.

Sonia stared at Lexy, a huge smile on her face. "Sorry if we've interrupted something. Max woke and was upset that he hadn't said goodnight to you. I should have texted first."

"No, no, it's fine." Lexy ran a hand down her hair. "I'll call you tomorrow."

"Okay. Have fun." There was a definite throaty chuckle from Sonia before the connection terminated.

Lexy put down the phone and closed her eyes for a brief second. She sensed Daniel come to stand in front of her.

"When were you going to tell me?" A muscle pulsed in his jaw.

"I don't know."

"Is this something you do? Were you hoping to get pregnant with my kid and then hit me up for child support? What's the matter, your first baby daddy wasn't rich enough?" The vile accusation spewed from the lips that had been bringing her pleasure only moments before.

She leapt to her feet, forgetting she hadn't fastened his shirt, which gapped open. "No! I'd never do that. How could you even think it?"

"Trust me, *cherie*"—she flinched at the disdainful way he said the endearment—"you wouldn't be the first woman who's tried that little game with me. And by your own admission your mother deliberately got pregnant to snare your father. Perhaps the plum hasn't rolled so far from the orchard."

"How dare you. You know nothing about me." She pulled the shirt tighter around her and crossed her arms over her chest.

"*Apparemment*. We have spent the past forty-eight hours together and not once have you mentioned that you have a child."

"Well, I do. A little boy named Max. He's three years old and the love of my life."

"And his father?" So help her, if he kept looking down his nose at her like that, she'd punch him. He could show up for the race in Russia with a nice shiner, compliments of his "chaperone."

"Is out of my life. For good. And for your information, I never once asked him for a penny in child support."

"So where's your son now?"

"My friend Sonia is looking after him. The twenty thousand pounds Mr. Petersen mentioned is for child care."

"You left your son. For eight weeks. For twenty grand. What kind of mother are you?"

She snapped. A red haze replaced his beautiful features. Not until Daniel held both her fists and sat her back down on the sofa did she realize she'd been repeatedly punching him on the chest.

A rueful smile twisted up one corner of his mouth. "I'm sorry. I shouldn't have said that." There was a hint of remorse in his tone. Enough to deflate her anger.

"I'll tell you what kind of mother I am." Tears now streamed down her face, landing on Daniel's hands where they still held hers. "I'm a desperate one. It was either come with you, leaving Max behind, or lose my job. And I can't afford that. I have nothing in savings to tide me over until I can get a new position. And my friend Sonia is looking after Max. She has a son the same age. And her husband just lost his job, so the money is really helping them out…" She couldn't say any more as sobs wracked her body.

Daniel pulled her against his chest. His hands ran up and down her back, his shirt no barrier to the comforting embrace. When she eventually quieted, he said, "So, because of this stupid photo of me and Jacqueline, I've taken a mother away from her young son."

"You could explain about the photo," she murmured against his bare skin. Then she could get out of his arms, go home, and never know what it would have been like between them.

He released her and stood. "No. That's not an

option. But I won't be the reason you have to be apart from your son. He'll just have to come with us."

***

Daniel stared out the window as they taxied down the small runway. They were once again strapped into the leather seats of Jacques's plane, headed back to London. Lexy had called her friend and explained the situation so Max would be ready for their arrival.

Dieu, she had a child. It was a complication in the next eight weeks he hadn't expected. It was bad enough he was distracted by her. Lexy got him. She understood his career, his focus, and dedication, was able to talk intelligently about the things that mattered to him and life in general. And to top all that, she was as sexy as a concept car, and she made him laugh more than anyone in recent years. But she had a kid. Children were a definite line never to be crossed where he was concerned. Then Lexy made a snuffly sound, and the pain on her face caused an ache in his own chest. He was so screwed.

"I'm not sure if Max is going to be happy to see me," she said, her voice raw.

"Why the hell not? You're his mother; of course he's going to be happy." Daniel may not have known a mother's love personally, but he could recognize it when he saw it. It was one of the reasons he'd insisted her son come with them. Nothing and no one, especially him, should keep a loving parent and child apart.

The other reason was that having a kid around was the ultimate abstinence incentive. Last night had been amazing, up to the point when her phone rang. He'd never felt such an emotional connection with a woman before. It had the power to destroy him. But with her toddler in tow, there'd be no more sexy times. He could focus entirely on the track now. *Merde*, at least he hoped so. More likely he'd die of blue balls syndrome. Even the hint of tears in Lexy's voice wasn't the turn-off it usually was. He fought the urge to take her in his arms and comfort her.

Lexy blew her nose before replying. "Sonia's husband, Mark, has been taking the boys to the park to play football. This is the first time Max has had a father figure to do stuff like that with him. I'm worried he won't want to leave this taste of a real family to come with me." She looked away and nibbled on the side of her index finger.

Women. He thought she'd be happy she didn't have to leave her son behind. "You are a real family. I was raised with my half brother by a man I'm not even related to. But they're my family. What makes a family is love."

At least that elicited a watery smile. "I've got that covered then. I love him so much. I worry constantly that I'm not doing enough, don't spend enough time with him. He won't have the same opportunities if he stays with me. But I can't give him up…"

"Why on earth would you give him up? What's really happening here, Lexy?"

She pulled in a shuddering breath. "Nothing. Sorry,

I'm just being paranoid. If my boss, or anyone really, knows that Max is with us, I could lose my job and custody. That would destroy me."

"Why? Do you have some kind of court order stopping you from taking your son out of the country?" This was getting more complicated by the minute. Why hadn't she told him any of this last night? Not that he'd given her a lot of time to talk after his announcement. He'd been so angry that she'd kept a huge part of herself hidden while he'd wanted to tell her all his secrets, he'd walked away. Now, in the light of day, he could see he hadn't really been fair. But his brain had been deprived of blood for so long it hadn't been working rationally.

"No. Max's father doesn't know he has a son. And I have to keep it that way."

Maybe my mother never told my father about me. Maybe the guy trying to contact me really does just want to meet me once before he dies. But his situation was different. He was beyond the need for a father. Why was Lexy keeping her son from his?

"Who is Max's father?"

She looked away. "No one important. He's an American, from Texas, so when we go there it's essential that Max be kept away from the media."

"What aren't you telling me, Lexy?"

Her hands twisted in her lap. "Max's father is my ex-husband. He left me before I knew I was pregnant. But if he finds out I had his son … well, let's just say he's not the type of man who would share custody."

"How did you hide your pregnancy during your

divorce proceedings?"

"That was all done through lawyers. I just signed where I was told. I didn't want a cent from Wesley. I just wanted to put the whole thing behind me."

"But you have a constant reminder of your marriage in your son."

"Max was the only good thing to come out of that relationship. I gave up everything for him. And I love him so much. It's only right I should get to keep him."

"What do you mean?"

"At my nineteen-week scan, the doctors discovered that there was something wrong with Max's heart. They weren't even sure if he was going to survive the birth. I quit university and concentrated on keeping my baby alive, going on bedrest for the whole last half of my pregnancy. I used all the money my father had set aside for me for school."

"But Max is okay?" Lexy was a strong woman to cope with that alone. No wonder she was adamant about keeping her son.

"At thirty-two weeks' gestation his heart rate dropped suddenly, so they performed an emergency C-section. He was in the neonatal intensive care unit for six months." Her voice broke and again he experienced prickles of pain in his chest. He should get the F1 doctor to check him out before he hit the track next week.

"That must have been really hard. Did your mother help?"

"No. It was just me and Max. One night they let me hold him, as they didn't think he was going to make it through to the morning. I was at rock bottom, holding my dying baby. I promised him, and I promised myself, that I was going to do everything in the world to keep him safe and be the best damned mother a child ever had. I kept saying over and over to the top of his head. 'Live for me, Max, and I'll live for you.' He kept up his end of the bargain so I have to do the same."

"Does he still have heart problems?"

"Actually, the next day he got a heart transplant. Someone else's tragedy saved us. Max suffers from asthma, but the doctors are hopeful that he'll grow out of it. He's my miracle baby. He gave me something to live for when I had nothing."

Lexy went back to chewing on her finger.

Daniel resumed his contemplation of the rapidly passing countryside beneath them. *Would I be different if my mother had loved me so fiercely? What if I was really the playboy everyone imagines and I discovered I had a child somewhere? If I discover who Lexy's ex-husband is, should I tell him he has a child?* This was precisely the kind of mental distraction he did not need in his life right now. He could almost feel the championship slipping from his grasp.

With the short flight over, they were soon in a taxi trudging their way through London's traffic. Eventually they arrived at a small terraced house, the outside clean but in need of a paint job. They were barely on the path before the door flew open and a little boy with a dark mop of hair and bright blue eyes launched himself at Lexy.

"Mummy, Mummy!" he screamed excitedly.

She picked him up and hugged him so tightly the boy squirmed to draw a breath. On seeing Daniel, Max tucked his face into Lexy's neck for protection. At the door stood a heavily pregnant woman, her tall, thin husband, and another boy a little larger than Max.

"Hi, I'm Daniel Michaud." He held out his hand first to the man staring at him as though Prince Harry had just shown up to knight the family dog. The woman, who must be Sonia, narrowed her eyes.

"Mark Connors, and this is my wife, Sonia, and our son, Andrew. I'm a huge fan."

"Of me or F1?"

"Well, the sport. But now that I've met you…"

"I'll try to earn your support. Lexy tells me Max considers you his extended family. He's a lucky boy to have so many people love him."

"He's a great lad. Do you have time for a cup of tea?" Sonia finally spoke.

"We really—" Lexy began. They'd hoped to make a quick turnaround and get back to France as soon as possible. He had a sponsor event he was supposed to attend tonight in Paris.

"Of course," Daniel replied. He could tell that Sonia wasn't sure about this change of plans by the way she glared at him.

They all went into a compact sitting room packed with toys. A small suitcase stood against the wall. Max still had his face tucked under Lexy's chin and his chubby arm wrapped around her neck. A neck that last night Daniel had admired for its graceful elegance as he trailed kisses down to her shoulder. This going back to strictly colleagues thing sucked.

Sonia bustled off to the kitchen to make the tea, and Lexy, after putting Max down, excused herself to grab a few things she'd forgotten from her flat upstairs. That left Daniel with the two boys and Mark. When the other man stood, the sweat broke out on Daniel's forehead. Children were like spiders, best viewed from a distance.

"I'll help Sonia," Mark excused himself.

He was alone with the boys, both of whom eyed him warily. Give him a car going 300 kilometers per hour on a damp track with his tires losing grip any day. That sort of danger he could face. What if one of them started to cry?

Then he spotted a small metal car wedged under the sofa cushion and pulled it out. A Lamborghini Aventador. "I have one of these in life size," he said. Andrew didn't look impressed, but Max finally turned his blue eyes on Daniel.

"What color?" Max asked, his head cocked to one side, as if Daniel's answer could make the difference between them being friends or mortal enemies.

"Red."

The little boy released what sounded like an Italian term of disgust. "Ferraris are red. Lambos should be lellow."

Lellow? Mon Dieu, this child was priceless. "You're right. But they didn't have a yellow one and I was desperate. Maybe I could have it painted?"

Max nodded as though that were an acceptable solution. It might be okay. This kid was all right, which shouldn't be a surprise since he was Lexy's son.

"What other cars do you have?" Max took a step closer, whereas Andrew started to pull the leaves off a potted plant. As the only adult in the room, should he stop him? No way was Daniel going to risk tears over some foliage. He'd send Sonia a new plant.

"I've got a Ferrari, in the proper red, a green McLaren, a blue Aston Martin, a white Koenigsegg, a black Bugatti, and, of course, my silver Mercedes."

Max came right up to him and put his tiny hand on Daniel's knee. "Can I see them?"

"Of course. They're at my brother's house in France."

Lexy appeared in the doorway and Max rushed over to her. "We have to go right now. The man said I can see his cars. He's got a Bugatti." Max said it as *boo-cat-ee*. Daniel was going to call it that from now on.

She knelt down in front of her son and straightened his hair. "We'll leave in a few minutes, Max. Don't you want to say goodbye to Andrew? We're going to be gone for a long time."

"Bye, Andrew." Max tugged on his mother's hand again, trying to pull her out the door.

"Max." The warning tone in Lexy's voice made Daniel straighten in his chair.

"Oh, all right. Grown-ups don't understand." He plopped down on the carpet and ran the toy Lambo along the coffee table.

Mark and Sonia returned with a tea tray laden with four types of biscuits. Both boys looked pleadingly at their mothers but didn't dive for the plate of cookies when it was set down. Cars made Max impatient, but evidently biscuits he could wait for.

"When is your baby due?" Daniel asked as Sonia lowered herself into a chair.

"Eight weeks and it can't come soon enough. Andrew was three weeks early, though, so the doctor thinks this baby might be as well."

Small talk centered around babies and things he had absolutely no knowledge of, but he must have asked the right questions and nodded in the right places, because by the time he'd finished his tea Sonia gave him a friendly smile.

There were lots of hugs and kisses and wishes for safe trips. Andrew was pulled away from denuding the greenery to say his farewells. Daniel, Lexy, and Max climbed into the taxi, and Lexy was strapping her son into his car seat when the boy began to squirm.

"Wait, we can't go without Dude. We have to bring him with us."

"Max, that's not possible," Lexy tried to reason with him. "Sonia and Andrew will look after him."

"No, no, no. He has to come. I can't sleep without saying goodnight to him."

The more Lexy tried to convince Max that Dude, whatever that was, had to stay, the more hysterical Max became. Tears streamed down his face, which was red with his exertion in trying to convince his mother. It was probably just some giant teddy bear the kid was particularly attached to. They had a private plane; no reason the boy couldn't have his favorite toy.

"Of course Dude can come," Daniel said, as Lexy looked at the point of losing it.

"Yay!" Max cheered. The tears stopped instantly and a huge smile covered the boy's face. Had he just been played? By a three-year-old?

"I'll go get him. Where is he?" Daniel offered.

"On the kitchen counter, upstairs in our flat." There was an odd light in Lexy's eyes as she handed him her keys.

Two minutes later he knew why. Dude was a fish.

Chapter Seven

She had to give it to him, Daniel was a great sport. He'd come back from her flat carrying Dude the betta fish in his bowl like a treasured pet, and then held it for the whole flight. Including the rough landing, which ended with a decidedly wet spot right in his crotch. And he hadn't complained once or rolled his eyes at Max's continual chatter. Two hours of three-year-old questions had tested her limits as a mother.

"Can I see your cars now?" Max asked as soon as they arrived at the chateau. He didn't comment on the size of the house or the luxurious grounds.

"Sure. Let me just find a spot for Dude. Do you want him in your room?" Daniel made no mention of needing to change his trousers.

"I share a room with Mummy," Max said. "Is it big enough for Dude, too?"

"We have lots of bedrooms. You don't have to share with your mummy. You could have your own room. You and Dude." Daniel's eyes lingered on her lips and a warm flush spread from her neck down. Maybe if Max had his own room…

Damn it, no. That ship sailed last night with Max's ill-timed call. She was back to mum mode. Sexy Lexy had to get back in her bottle and wait another few years, or decades. God, what kind of mother was she that she wanted to roll back time, skip the call from her son, and have one night with Daniel? She had what she wanted from the beginning—not to be parted from Max. It was more than enough. Had to be.

"No, I have to stay with Mummy because she has bad dreams sometimes. Some man named Wesley is being mean to her." Oh God, did she talk in her sleep? She'd never mentioned Max's father to him. But it made sense now why her son always asked the name of every man they met. He was on the lookout for the Wesley who was mean to her.

Daniel knelt down so he was at Max's eye level. "I understand. Just so you know, no man is going to be mean to your mum while I'm around." The two males shared a nod of mutual acknowledgment. She was to be protected. Max certainly hadn't inherited that from his father.

"How about I find a place for Dude and you two boys go see the cars?" Lexy suggested. She took the fish bowl from Daniel's hands, lingering in the exchange, holding his gaze in an effort to communicate how much she appreciated him treating her son like a person and not an inconvenience. When Max reached up to take Daniel's hand, her heart fibrillated. Was she dangling more of the impossible in front of her son? She'd have to make sure Max understood this was only a temporary arrangement, and Daniel wouldn't have a permanent place in their lives.

If she weren't careful, she wouldn't be the only one to lose her heart to Daniel Michaud. Whoa, hold the phone. Her heart had to keep well clear of that stupidity. But seeing him walk away, holding her son's hand, talking cars and promising to protect her, it was damned hard to remember he was an international playboy just waiting for the next available woman to pass by.

She hurried to put Dude in her room, giving him a few shakes of food Daniel'd had the foresight to grab as well. Should she follow them to the garage? Or give them space and wait for their return?

As she dithered in the hallway, Marie the housekeeper approached her. "*Mademoiselle* Lexy, Daniel said you would need an *au pair* to help look after your son while you travel. I called my niece who is a teacher, and she is here if you'd like to meet her."

"Of course. Thank you."

"Would you like to interview her in the *petit salon*? She's waiting now in the kitchen."

"Oh, I'll just come down to the kitchen with you." Or wasn't that the done thing in a house like this? Hanging out with Daniel should come with a manual. "Unless, of course, you don't want people in your kitchen."

Marie beamed. "The kitchen is fine. Follow me."

The kitchen was not what she was expecting. Neither was the woman at the long wooden table cradling a cup of coffee. The room was bright and airy, painted a sunny yellow and full of knickknacks and photos of Daniel and, she assumed, his brother Jacques as a child. It was the kind of kitchen a mother would cook in. Not a servant in a big house.

And the woman waiting for her looked nothing like

any teacher Lexy had ever had. Her blond hair fell in a pure glossy sheet to her waist. Large, gray eyes stared out of the face of an angel. She was even more beautiful than Lexy's mother had been in her time.

"*Mademoiselle* Lexy, please allow me to introduce you to my niece, Genevieve Dubois."

Genevieve stood and Lexy forced a smile on her face. For God's sake, why did the woman have to be tall and slim as well? Next to her, Lexy'd look like the also ran. But she wasn't here to compete in a beauty pageant. She had a job to do and needed help to do it. No one could find out Max was with them. This was so complicated.

"I am pleased to meet you, *mademoiselle*," Genevieve began. Her English was perfect. Max would have no difficulty understanding her.

"Please, call me Lexy. And you, too, Marie." The older woman just nodded then bustled about the kitchen making tea and coffee.

"You're not currently teaching?" Lexy asked as Genevieve resumed sitting.

"No. I was teaching abroad last year and I had a traumatic experience. I've not been able to go back into the classroom. But *ma tante* thought that perhaps if I only had one child to keep safe, it might be better for me."

Keep safe? That was an odd choice of words. Surely her job was to teach. The haunted look in her eye stilled Lexy's tongue. Yet there was a gentleness about the woman that set her at ease. "Max is a good boy, but he does need to be watched closely. He has a tendency towards mischief. Are you sure you're up to it after your, um, experience?"

"I believe so. I understand you're not leaving for a few days. Perhaps I could have a test period and see how we get on. I have a friend who would also be available if I can't manage. I have to try something. At the moment I have too much time to think."

Lexy knew that feeling. How many hours had she sat beside Max's NICU bed thinking? Her son had given her something to live for, so perhaps he could help in Genevieve's healing. "As Daniel is paying the bills, I'll have to ask him."

"Ask him what?" Daniel said as he appeared in the doorway, carrying Max. Her son had his head on Daniel's shoulder and was fighting to keep his eyes open. Without waiting for her to reply, Daniel greeted the other woman. "Genevieve, how good to see you. How are you doing? Better?"

"A little."

Daniel touched Genevieve's shoulder in a show of support. But aside from that there was no hint he was interested in the woman. Instead his hot gaze roved over Lexy, lingering on her lips. "Is the question you want to ask whether I think Genevieve would be a perfect person to look after Max while you're busy? If so, the answer is yes. I asked Marie to call her this morning before we left." He stroked Max's arm until her boy raised his head. "Max, this is my friend Genevieve. She's going to help look after you while your mum is working. Okay?"

"She's bootiful," Max said before returning his

head to Daniel's shoulder. God, Max was so like his grandfather. If her father showed up at the next race, she'd introduce him to his grandson. It was time to mend fences. Max deserved to have a man in his life, and she could use a father again.

"As bootiful as the Boo-cat-ee?" Daniel teased.

"No, but she's a girl, not a car."

Daniel laughed. "We'll work on your priorities when you get older, my friend."

"Here, Max, come with me. I'll show you where I put Dude." Lexy reached for her son, but he tightened his arm around Daniel's neck.

"No. I want to stay with Daniel."

She expected a horrified look from Daniel, but instead she saw an indulgent smile. "I have to go to a boring party, Max. And you need to get your rest if you're going for a drive in every one of my cars tomorrow." He handed Max to her, who snuggled into her neck and started to snore within seconds.

Daniel sure knew the way to Max's heart. Was her own in jeopardy, too?

***

Daniel slipped into the library, careful not to disturb Lexy who was curled up with a book on the sofa. The flames from the gas fireplace danced light across her features. A plastic receiver sat on the coffee table next to her, the background white noise not disturbing her concentration. For a moment he just stared. She was so beautiful. And seeing her interact with her son this afternoon had created a queer feeling in his gut.

He tossed his tuxedo jacket onto the chair beside her and she jumped with a startled gasp.

"Oh, Daniel, I didn't think you'd be home until the wee hours. Max went right to sleep, and Genevieve's gone home to pack. She'll be back in the morning." She shut her book and moved as though to leave.

"Please, don't go. Not yet. I just want to talk." Well, that was a bare-assed lie, but he'd stick to his word.

She sank back into the sofa and curled her feet under her. To resist touching her, he sat on the chair where he'd thrown his jacket.

"How was the party?" She ran her hand over her cheek and tucked a stray strand of hair behind her ear. Exactly the path his lips longed to take.

"It was okay. After a while they're all the same." He'd expected to enjoy being back in his element. In control—hiding behind his playboy mask. Not floundering in desire for a woman he shouldn't want, excited to show her son his car collection. Instead, he'd found himself listening for Lexy's laugh and looking around to see where Max had got to.

"Did you at least get photographed with a woman?"

He searched her eyes. Was she really trying to set him up?

"Not sure. There were a lot of women and a lot of cameras. I'm sure something will show up in the press." In reality he'd barely spent half an hour at the party. He'd met his contractual obligations and exited.

The rest of the evening he'd spent at his apartment in Paris. Alone. Wondering when his life had become so complicated. He needed to keep his focus on the next five races, on winning the championship. It had to be the novelty of his situation that intrigued him. He'd never spent much time around kids. And when Jacques and Maya came out of hiding, he'd probably have a handful of nieces and nephews to interact with. So he'd decided to give himself until he boarded the plane for Russia to relax and enjoy the change of pace.

"I still have your shirt," Lexy said softly, a faint blush tingeing her cheeks with pink.

If she wanted to keep her clothes on now, she shouldn't remind him of how her dark nipples had shown through the thin fabric. He yanked off his tie. "Keep it. I've got plenty of others."

She was biting the side of her finger again. "Daniel … about last night."

Dieu, why did women always want to get into the gory details? "What about it?"

"I don't want you to think I only wanted to have sex with you because you're a playboy racer. It was the guy who taught me to drive and laughed at my jokes I wanted to be intimate with."

That hit him between the eyes. He had to clear his throat before he could answer. "Good to know."

"And I didn't tell you about Max because, as selfish as it seems, I just wanted to be a woman for a few weeks."

"I'm pretty sure even mothers get to have sex now and again. Otherwise, there'd be a lot of only children around. You're a mother, not a martyr. Turning yourself into one isn't going to help your son."

She glanced at him then, her eyes flashing anger. "I'm not being a martyr. And I can't just switch off being a mother. It's not a job. It's who I am."

"It should be part of who you are, not your whole being. Otherwise you risk losing yourself. And then what will you do when Max grows up and leaves home?"

"Who's the psychologist today?"

He sat back in the chair. He hadn't meant for this to be a confrontation. He just wanted her to enjoy herself. And maybe him. "Will you try over the next two months to do one thing each day that is just for you?"

She stared at him as though the idea was completely foreign to her. "Why? Why do you care?"

"I just do." *And let's not psychoanalyze that, please.*

"But Max—"

"Is not here right now." His gaze drifted down to the swell of her breasts. His mouth watered. So much for her kid proving to be an abstinence incentive.

"But he's here." Lexy put her hand on her heart. "You're on a fast track to being his hero. He's car-obsessed and your whole life revolves around them. If he gets the vibe that there's anything other than just a professional relationship between us, he'll be devastated when we both go back to our separate lives at the end of the season."

He nodded. Hurting Max would be unforgivable.

But he wasn't sure he'd be able to hide his, um, "interest" in Lexy.

"So what do we do?"

"Ignore this chemistry between us." The heat in her gaze as it roamed over him belied her words.

"Not going to happen."

She threw her hands in the air. "For God's sake, can't you tone down the playboy routine?"

"It's not the playboy who wants to kiss every inch of your body, making you writhe and scream with pleasure. I may be many things, Lexy, but at the base of them all I'm a man who wants you. This isn't going to go away just because you say so."

Her eyelids closed for a moment and another blush colored her skin. When she opened her eyes again there was resignation but also a hint of excitement in them. "Can we at least agree that if Max is around we're hands off, colleagues only?"

"I'm willing to play that game." And several others he had in mind. "Let's start now. I believe it's your move."

She rose from the sofa, put both hands on the arm of his chair, and leaned in. She'd had a glass of wine after dinner, the scent lingering on her breath mingling with her flowery perfume and the essential essence that was all Lexy. "I'll probably regret this. But at the moment I can't think why." Her voice was husky. When she licked her lips his internal temperature skyrocketed.

"Don't think. Just feel." *'Cause that's what I'm doing.*

He threaded a hand in her hair to bring her head down, his other palm already cupping her breast. When their mouths were a mere millimeter apart, a wail came screeching through the plastic receiver. “Mummy! Where are you?”

Lexy straightened with a resigned sigh. “My son and his perfect timing.”

Before he could wish her a good night, she was gone.

And so was any hope he had of getting to sleep anytime soon.

***

Lexy pulled her ringing mobile phone from her pocket as she searched for Max and Daniel. They’d disappeared after lunch, and it was time for Max’s nap.

“Yes, hello?” She answered without bothering to look at the caller display.

“Alexandra.”

Bloody hell. What did her boss want now? He’d already emailed her several times to make sure she was getting along with the client’s golden boy. If he knew just how close to “getting along” they were, he’d probably have a heart attack. At least Max’s constant presence had prevented any further slip-ups in her newly discovered sexuality. But, man, was it hard to be with Daniel all day long and not jump his bones.

“Mr. Petersen, how are you?”

“Wondering what’s going on. You’ve been with”—God, she wished he hadn’t used that term —

"Daniel for five days now and not a single photo of him with a woman has appeared in the press."

"Um, yes, I know. It's just that he's between races so he's been hanging out at his brother's house. And the photographers at the party he was at on Saturday must have missed him before he left with … a woman."

"Not good enough. You need to restore his playboy image. Take him to a club or something. Whatever it is you young people do to waste time."

"It's Monday, Mr. Petersen. No one goes clubbing on a Monday."

"Make an exception. If there are fewer people there, it's more likely he'll be seen. Use your womanly charms. Tell him you need to get out."

"I'll do my best." *Misogynistic old bat. I should report him to HR.* Use her womanly charms. For God's sake, it was the twenty-first century. The problem was that the way she wanted to use her womanly charms wouldn't result in Daniel being seen with another woman.

Talk about a conflict of interest. She'd thought she'd at least be able to rely on Daniel reverting to his playboy persona in public. This assignment was going to be more work than she imagined. And, given her personal interest, possibly one of the hardest things she'd ever done. Was there some reason Daniel hadn't been photographed with a woman on Saturday? Did it involve his still-unexplained relationship with Jacqueline?

Mr. Petersen's nasally voice interrupted her musing. "I'll expect a photo on the internet by tomorrow. Or perhaps I need to find someone else to take your place. That girl on reception seemed keen."

Asshole doesn't even know the name of his receptionist.

"I'll take care of it. And we leave for Russia tomorrow, so the media coverage should pick up once the practice sessions start."

"I'll be watching." And with that he hung up.

His parting words sent a shiver down her spine. Thankfully, Max had taken quickly to Genevieve, although he called her Vivi. So, with a bit of luck on their side, they'd be able to keep him out of the spotlight.

"Marie, have you seen Daniel and Max?" Lexy asked the housekeeper as she passed.

"I took cookies and milk into the *petit salon* about half an hour ago for them. Your little boy is an angel. I hope that soon this house will be filled with many children. It has been too long…"

Well, they wouldn't be Lexy's children. But she didn't want to deflate the housekeeper's good mood. "Thanks, I'll look for them there."

There was no sound coming from inside the *petit salon* when she arrived; which, where Max was concerned, was a sure sign that she wasn't going to like what she saw when she opened the door.

Slipping quietly into the room, she stood staring for a long moment until emotion clogged her throat and the tears threatened to fall. Daniel lay on the sofa, Max sprawled on top of him, both of them fast asleep. Max had a toy car clutched in one hand, his other fisted on

Daniel's t-shirt. Daniel's arms were wrapped around her son, keeping him safe. She took a couple of photos with her phone, wanting to cherish this memory.

Maybe even after the racing season was over Daniel could still be part of their lives. He could pop over to their flat in London and … what? Try to fit his six-foot length onto her tiny sofa? She wasn't delusional enough to believe that would ever happen. At the end of the season Daniel would go back to his life and she to hers. The photo would be all that remained.

Genevieve waved at her from the doorway, so Lexy tiptoed over.

"I offered to take Max, but Daniel said to leave him. He also told me to remind you about what he said on Saturday night."

She assumed he was referring to her promise to "do one thing for herself" and not the implication that that one thing would be him. It was pouring rain so that ruled out a walk around the gardens. There was a huge claw-foot bathtub in her en suite bathroom. When was the last time she'd had a soak in bubbles? This side of never.

"Thanks, Genevieve. I'm going to have a bath. Will you look after Max when he wakes?"

"But of course."

Lexy had achieved prune-level of wrinkledness when there was a soft knock on the bathroom door. Arranging the remaining bubbles strategically, she called, "Come in," expecting either Marie or Genevieve. The knock was too quiet to be Max.

Daniel entered, his eyes blazing with desire when he saw her lying in the tub, barely covered by the bubbles. He held a glass of red wine, accompanied by a smile that could evaporate the water in the tub.

"Glad to see you're taking my advice. I have it on good authority, though, that bubble baths require a glass of wine for complete enjoyment."

She was pretty sure complete enjoyment would come from sharing the bath with him. But lying here naked, and sober, she was too shy to suggest it.

"I was just about to get out."

"Don't let me stop you."

"Daniel." She used her firm mother's voice, but he just smiled in return.

"Lexy." He mimicked her tone as he handed her the wine glass and then leaned against the sink. "I've already seen you mostly naked, or don't you remember?"

Oh, she remembered all right. In fact, her body was clamoring for a reenactment. She was about to suggest that maybe he could scrub her back when a tiny body hurtled into the room yelling, "Bubbles!"

Daniel groaned. And for the first time since she became a mother, she wasn't happy to see her son.

"Bet you regret insisting he come along now, aren't you?" she asked with a laugh.

"You have no idea." He tousled Max's hair then left the room.

Actually, she did know.

Chapter Eight

The drivers' meeting was taking forever—the usual reminders to keep within the track limits, respect the blue flags, and cautioning about pit lane speeds. What, did they think they were all new to this? By this point in the season, even the rookies were checking their social media feeds, pretending to be listening.

He'd arrived in Russia two days earlier to acclimatize and go over a few things with his team. They'd made a couple of minor aerodynamic adjustments to the car since Japan, and he was eager to get behind the wheel and test them in free practice.

Annoyingly, he was even more eager to see Lexy, and, he had to admit, Max as well. Lexy, to appease her boss, had convinced him to let her take a photo of him holding Genevieve, which she then leaked to a gossip site. Within five minutes, speculation was all over his social media accounts about the new woman in his life. If only they knew it was the woman behind the camera and not the one in his arms.

Tonight was a big gala event, and he'd convinced Lexy that she had to attend with him. He almost rubbed his hands together at the chance to spend some time with her without her delightful son and his terrible timing.

At last the meeting was over and he could retreat to

the relative chaos of the team garage. There followed three more meetings with the team principal, his chief mechanic, and the PR person advising him which events he had to attend and the ones that would be nice if he made an appearance. Team sponsors trumped all, and showing at their parties was mandatory. At least there would be enough photo ops that hopefully he'd be able to keep Lexy's boss off her back.

Speaking of whom, Lexy, Max, and Genevieve should have arrived by now. He sneaked out the rear of the garage and scored a ride with one of the other drivers back to the hotel. He had to duck into his own room for ten minutes while a couple of F1 hangers-on had a chat in the hallway. Didn't these people know that bars and lobbies were for talking? Finally, the coast was clear and he made his way to Lexy's room, knocking gently in case Max was sleeping.

Lexy answered but before he could even step into the room, Max flung himself at Daniel's legs. *Don't get too used to this—it's only temporary.* With his arms full of wriggling boy, Lexy pulled him into the room and shut the door. He gave Max a tight hug and slipped him a toy car from his pocket before lowering the child to the floor. Excited, Max ran to Genevieve to show her his new treasure and explain to her all about the vehicle. There weren't many cars that boy didn't know. He was an automotive savant.

"I don't think anyone saw us arrive," Lexy said.

"And hello to you, too." It would've been nice if Lexy had thrown herself at him as well.

"Sorry; I'm on edge." She shook her head as if to

restart her brain. "How did your meetings go today? Did they get the new aero package working?" She tucked a loose strand of hair behind her ear; the rest was tightly restrained in a severe bun at the back of her head. His fingers itched to remove the pins and let the silky strands flow through his fingers as he kissed her. She chewed the side of her finger as she watched Max play.

He eased her hand away from her mouth, and, after making sure Max was absorbed in his new toy, kissed the tortured digit. "Relax; it'll be fine. If anyone asks, we'll hint that Max belongs to Genevieve. But most people here are so caught up in their own lives I doubt they'll even notice."

"You're right. I'm sorry—"

He kissed her then. Kissed her long, kissed her soft, kissed her hard. Kissed her until she clung to him, her fingers wound in his hair, her other hand on his back holding him as tightly as he was her. He kissed her like a starving man would devour his first meal in weeks.

"Max," she whispered against his lips as he pulled back fractionally to readjust his position.

"Is now in the other room with Genevieve." Smart woman. He'd have to add a bonus to her salary.

He lowered his head again, but Lexy put a hand on his chest. "Wait. I can't do this."

"Why not? Max isn't watching. I thought that's what we agreed. We can't take things all the way with your son in the next room, but we can at least have a taster."

"No, I won't be able to pretend there's nothing going on if we make out every time we're alone."

Biting back a frustrated groan, he temporarily halted his assault on her senses. He was back in his world now. Time they did things his way. "I'm just living up to my reputation. You made me into an international playboy. According to you, I live for the conquest."

"I don't count. Move on."

"We both know that's not an option. We have unresolved lust issues that neither of us is going to be able to ignore much longer."

"Daniel, please."

"That's what I'm trying to do—please you. Let's go back to my room for an hour or so. The reception isn't until eight." He trailed his lips from her ear down to the collar of her shirt, encouraged by the quiver that shot through her.

"Max—" Her protest was weakened by the moan that escaped her lips as he rubbed his thumb over her already-hard nipple.

"Is. With. Genevieve. That's what I'm paying her for, remember? To look after him."

"While I'm working."

"Or playing."

She put both her hands on his chest and pushed. Not sufficient to move him but enough to get her message across. "I can't do this right now."

He'd make a strategic retreat and try again later. "All right. The reception for my team sponsor is in the main ballroom. Meet me there at eight."

Without waiting for her to object, he left the room and headed for a cold shower.

He needed all of his focus if he wasn't going to crash in the first corner melee on Sunday. If he didn't deal with this frustration and distraction, he could kiss the championship goodbye right now.

Damn that woman. He had to get her out of his system before the race. He'd make love to her and be done with it. It was time to put all that playboy practice into action.

***

Lexy stepped into the noisy ballroom, scanning it for her father. Who was she kidding? She was looking for Daniel. Tonight was going to be a real test of her mettle. Could she watch him flirt with and seduce other women and not rugby tackle them? She was about to see the real Daniel Michaud. This was truly his world, where he ruled as king.

A tuxedo-clad waiter passed by and she snagged a glass of sparkling wine so she at least looked like she belonged. She took a sip. *Blecch*, Russian. No wonder almost everyone's glasses were still full. At least she wasn't in danger of getting drunk and throwing herself at Daniel. Her body still hummed from his kisses and caresses in her hotel room. Maybe if she laid claim to him first, he wouldn't have to flirt with other women. Except, wasn't that exactly what she was supposed to ensure? There was only so much aggravation a woman could take. Wanting one thing and having to do the exact opposite was tearing her apart.

A draught of air blew across her naked shoulders. She wished she hadn't listened to Genevieve and had brought her wrap with her. Max had cheerfully waved her goodnight, telling her she looked "bootiful" before returning his attention to the book Genevieve was reading to him. A pang of jealousy had shot through her. Reading the bedtime story was her job.

The hairs on the back of her neck stood on end and a tingle invaded her nerve endings. Even before he spoke, she knew Daniel was near. "You are magnificent," he said in her ear. She could feel the heat from his body wrap around her from behind. She was no longer chilled. It took every ounce of strength she possessed not to lean back into him. "This is very nice. The color suits you. But I'm still waiting to see you in the blue dress."

As she turned around, the satin of her brown gown slid against her skin like a caress. As nice as it felt, she wished it were Daniel's hands and lips on her. This line of thought was going to end up with her in a dark corner somewhere, her photo splashed all over the internet. She closed her eyes to try to gather her scattered brain cells, but the image of Daniel in his dark suit, pure white shirt, and green tie wouldn't be banished. She'd seen hundreds of photos of him in formal attire while working on the initial advertising campaign, so she should have been immune. But no photo could capture the sheer power and charisma he exuded. Now, if they could package that…

"I'm saving the blue dress for your victory party on

Sunday."

"Then I'm going to win the race just to see you wear it." His eyes devoured her. This wasn't going to work. One look at them and people would know something was going on between them. Unless this was how he looked at every woman.

"You'll win the race to solidify your position in the championship." God, why was her voice so breathless?

"That's the line I'll tell everyone. You and me, we'll know the truth." His gaze roved over her again, lingering on the swell of her breasts under the satin fabric. International Playboy Daniel was in high gear. "Are you sure you don't want to go up to my room? I could plead a headache."

Tempting. But she had a job to do, even though she hated it. "And miss my first F1 party?" She put a couple of feet distance between them.

"Haven't you been to one of these before?"

"No. I was too young to attend the evening events. My parents used to go out every night, though. I'd be left in the room with the hotel babysitter. Most of the time they only spoke the local language."

"Did you resent that? Being left behind, I mean?"

"No. Mum would dress up and look like a princess. It was one of the few times she was happy. Dad looked so handsome in his suits. And I learned a lot of languages from my babysitters."

"Now you're the princess who gets to go to the balls." His gaze roved over her again. Man, was it hot in here or what?

"More like Cinderella who gets to hang out at the

parties and make sure Prince Charming dances with all the real princesses."

His jaw clenched and a muscle jumped in his cheek. "Come meet my team."

He put his hand on her back and steered her toward a group of people. Many she recognized from watching F1 races on the telly. All greeted her warmly. She ruthlessly shut down the sensation that she was getting her family back. She couldn't go through the withdrawals again. She had to remember it was her and Max. Period.

"Hey, everyone," Daniel said. "This is Lexy. She's representing Destin Designs and is supposed to make sure I don't get into any trouble."

"Ha, ha, good luck with that, Lexy," one of the mechanics said.

"It will be a trial. But someone has to do it." She let out a weary sigh that made the group laugh.

"You look familiar. Have you been around F1 before?" Alan Stewart asked. He'd been a driver when she knew him; now he was a consultant with Daniel's team.

"Good memory. I was this high"—she put her hand at hip level—"when you knew me before. My last name is Camparelli." She waited for the explosion and wasn't disappointed.

"Oh my God, you're Alexandra Camparelli!" Therein followed lots of hugs, and comments along the lines of, "I knew you were going to grow up to be a beauty." Daniel mouthed, "I told you so," while one of the men gave her a hug.

"Does your father know you're here?" Alan asked. "And with Daniel Michaud?"

"Hey, I resemble that remark," Daniel protested.

Lexy let out a brittle laugh. The closer it got, the more anxious she was about her reunion with her father. What if he didn't welcome her with open arms? What if he turned his back on her? "No, he doesn't. And I'd really appreciate it if you'd let me surprise him."

"Just make sure Jean Lefebre is around when you do it. Wouldn't want Gian-Franco to have another heart attack," someone said.

Her father had a heart problem? Her chest tightened and it was hard to pull in a breath. What if she'd lost him without making amends for the way they'd parted?

"Jean is the doctor contracted to Formula 1 to make sure all the drivers are fit to drive. He's Jacqueline's husband," Daniel clarified.

Jacqueline. The reason Lexy was here in the first place. A niggle of trepidation slid down her spine, bumping each vertebrae as it went.

"I am so glad you're back with us, Alexandra. Give my love to your mother when you next see her," Alan said before excusing himself from the group. She had no plans to see her mother any time soon. God, her family was such a mess. F1 did that to people. The highs were immense, but the lows unbearable for some.

As if sensing her shift in mood, Daniel put his arm around her waist. "Dance with me?"

"I don't think that's wise. I'm supposed to make

sure you're seen with other women."

"You are the only woman I see." His intense green eyes caught her gaze and she couldn't look away. She'd been so very wrong. A playboy didn't make love to every woman in the room. He made each woman feel like she was the only one he wanted.

Unable to deny him, or herself, she accompanied him to the dance floor and managed not to release a sigh of contentment as his arms came around her.

"Are you worried about meeting your father again?" His lips were against her temple and she closed her eyes, savoring the moment. This was probably just standard operating procedure for him. No one would notice anything different.

"A little. Things didn't go so well last time I saw him. The phrases, 'You never loved me' and 'I hate you' were screamed a lot. Now to learn he has a heart problem … what if he sees me and collapses? Or worse, turns his back on me?"

"I'm sure he won't. I've met him a few times and got the impression he's lonely. He'll be happy to have you and Max in his life."

He pulled her a fraction closer and nibbled on her ear. "I've put in an appearance now. We can leave anytime."

The slow song ended and was replaced by one with a faster tempo. At least the Russian band was better than the wine. She put a more respectable distance between her and Daniel, much to her body's annoyance. "We can't leave together. And we're doing a terrible job of convincing people we aren't a couple.

We have to find some other woman for you to leave with."

"*Pour l'amour de Dieu*, Lexy."

Damn it, why'd he have to be so difficult? Did he think this was easy for her? He could afford to walk away from his Destin Designs contract and do whatever he pleased. Or whoever. She wasn't so lucky. Pulling out of his arms, she found a spot in the corner of the ballroom from where she could see everyone. Eventually, Daniel joined her. She refused to look at his face.

"What about her? She's beautiful." Lexy pointed out a blond woman dressed in six square inches of fabric.

"She's too skinny, and she's got so much filler in her lips it would be like kissing a balloon. Plus, she's dressed like a prostitute. I have standards, you know." He almost huffed out his refusal.

Great, a picky playboy. Wasn't that an oxymoron or something?

"Okay, what about the brunette talking to the guy with the really bad toupée?"

"Her face is so full of Botox, if a mosquito bit her it would die on contact. I prefer a more natural woman."

Lexy scanned the room again. Natural was in short supply with this crowd. Dismissing the women who were obviously married or already hanging on the arm of some man left only about two dozen.

"Okay, her, the one in the elegant black dress, with dark hair, and blue eyes. She's beautiful, not too skinny, as natural as you're going to get in this group, and looks like she has a sense of humor."

"Her boobs are fake. Look, they don't even move when she laughs."

"God, you're choosy. I'm trying to get you a date, not find you a wife."

Something flashed across his eyes but was gone before she could define it. "That's not amusing."

This isn't fun for me, either.

"Fine. You want a naturally endowed, curvy woman, with wrinkles and style." She scanned the party again. "Oh, I've got her. The woman who just walked in, so she won't have seen us together. She's good-looking, natural, her boobs look real, and she's nicely dressed. My work here is done." Lexy forced a note of enthusiasm in her voice. Picking out one's replacement sucked even more than a Dyson.

"No."

She turned to stare up at him. He had that look in his eyes again. "No? She meets every single one of your criteria. What's wrong with her?"

He took her hand and kissed the back of it, holding her gaze. "She's not you."

Chapter Nine

When a man told you he didn't want to be with any other woman in the room, you ran. Or melted. That was Lexy's other option.

Thankfully he didn't follow, and she made it to her suite without meeting anyone who knew her. And then her body punished her the rest of the night by replaying the sound of Daniel's voice over and over again. Her first test and she'd failed. If she lost her job, would it be Daniel's fault or hers?

The next morning she powered up her laptop and scanned the gossip sites, with one eye open for images from the night before. Had Daniel hooked up with some woman, or had he escaped without getting his photo taken? At the very end of the report on last night's event was a small photo with the caption: *Has the playboy been played?* Daniel was staring with undisguised interest at the retreating figure of a woman in a chocolate brown dress. She enlarged the photo as much as she could, but it was impossible to tell that the woman was her. Unless you'd been at the party. Could she trust in the discretion of Daniel's team? They were the only ones who knew who she was. For now.

Her phone buzzed with an incoming message: *Blonde last week. Brunette this week. Keep up the good work.*

It wasn't even five a.m. in London. Why was Mr. Petersen up so early? He must be really paranoid about this campaign. What if he decided to check up on her personally?

There was a soft knock on the hotel room door and she raced to answer it. Max was still asleep due to the time change.

"Daniel." He was already dressed in his overalls, his green eyes distant when he glanced at her. He made no move to enter the room or even touch her.

"Here's your paddock pass. You've got all access. I'm going to be on the track most of the day, but if you need to get in touch with me, my team will be able to get a message through. I'll have the PR woman send you a list of all my scheduled appearances." He handed her the lanyard with the plastic pass dangling at the bottom and turned to leave.

"Wait."

He stopped but didn't look back.

"I had to leave. There's too much at stake to throw it all away on something with no future."

"Well, I'm the one paying the price with sleepless nights. I broke my number one rule and got involved with a woman during the race season. I have to concentrate on my car now. I'll see you around."

And he was gone.

He thought they were involved? This was so complicated. Most girls went through these scenarios during their teens. Although she had a failed marriage behind her, she was still a novice in the relationship department. And what exactly did "involvement" with

Daniel entail?

The questions plagued her all morning. After breakfast she and Genevieve took Max to a nearby children's park. Genevieve was tense and nervous, looking around constantly for signs of danger. Max's squeals of delight eventually drew a smile from his skittish nanny. Lexy, however, was thinking about what Daniel had said this morning, so much she nearly got knocked out by her son on the swings. Should she spend one night with him and get it over with? Or tell him to find someone else to conquer because they were colleagues and he had to respect that?

After lunch back in the suite, Genevieve picked up the access pass Daniel had left. "I'll take Max to the hotel pool until it's his nap time. You go to the track."

"I'm not sure Daniel wants to see me."

"The question is: what do you want?"

He had made her promise to do one thing each day for herself. She wanted to see him drive, and going to the track today when it was unlikely her father would be around yet meant she could absorb the atmosphere without worry. Lexy quickly changed into the animal print jumpsuit and kissed Max goodbye. Her son was so in love with Genevieve, he hardly noticed her leave. Damn, it would be bad enough that she was never going to be satisfied with her humdrum life when this was over. She felt alive for the first time in so long. She didn't need her son devastated as well. Although she was pretty sure a three-year-old's heartbreak could be cured with a new toy or a trip to the zoo.

Three of the other drivers' wives were in the lobby

and offered her a lift to the track. Within five minutes, despite the fact that they each spoke a different native language, they were laughing and giggling like best friends. “Tomorrow before qualifying, a bunch of us WAGs are going to get our hair done. The TV cameras love to spot us in the garages, and I swear my gray hairs multiply in HD,” Tara, one of the wives, said. If this woman had ever had a gray hair amongst her jet-black locks, Lexy’d eat one of Max’s toy cars. Evidently even beautiful women had their moments of insecurity.

“Sure, I’d love to come. But I’m not a wife or girlfriend. I’m working with Daniel.”

“Of course, sweetie. We believe you. Although I’ve never seen Daniel devour any of his other colleagues with his eyes the way he does you. And you were pretty cozy on the dance floor last night.” Mandy was married to Robert, Daniel’s teammate.

Heat engulfed Lexy’s face. “That was…” She wasn’t an accomplished enough liar to finish the sentence.

“Leave her alone, Mandy. When she watches the race on Sunday, she’ll know,” Louisa said.

“Know what?” Lexy had watched hundreds of F1 races in her life. What kind of epiphany did they expect her to have this time?

“If you’re in love with a man behind the wheel, you’ll feel every curve, every dip in the track, as though you were in the car yourself,” Mandy said.

“And you’ll hold your breath so much you may black out,” Louisa added.

"I have to put disgusting stuff on my nails so I don't bite them." Tara flashed her nails, bitten down to the quick. "It doesn't always work."

More tips for coping with the stress of watching the man you love hurtling around a race track at 300 kilometers an hour in a car with enough power to break orbit followed. She listened and nodded at the right moments without too much worry about needing their advice. She wasn't in love with Daniel. Sure, she might be a bit more invested in the race results because she had a personal stake in the game now. If Daniel won the championship, his advertising value would go through the roof.

Shit. Am I becoming a crass advertising exec who sees people as a commodity?

Then she spotted Daniel and his ad revenue potential didn't even register. One night. That's all she wanted. They could go back to being colleagues after that.

He was with two other men and one woman, staring at a monitor covered in squiggly lines—telemetry from the car's running that morning. They were focusing on one particular section of the data. Her father had once told her there were two types of drivers: Type one understood every nuance of the car and gave feedback as though he'd built it himself. Type two showed up when he was needed, got behind the wheel, and drove. Daniel was obviously a type one.

Her reflection must have showed in the monitor because he turned around mid-sentence.

"Hi," she said. She was well read, spoke five

languages, and that was the best she could do.

Daniel stared at her for a moment then glanced at his colleagues. The smile he gave her seemed forced. "Lexy, I'm glad you came." He must be saving the frosty reception for when they were alone. He introduced her to the few in the garage who hadn't been at the party the night before. "The car is handling great on all but one section of the track," he explained. "I want to walk that area to see if I can figure out what's different about that particular piece of tarmac."

She glanced down at her heeled shoes. After a six-kilometer walk around the circuit in these shoes, walking barefoot across hot coals would be a welcome relief.

"Sure. Have you got a bottle of water for me? It's getting hot." Or maybe it was the way he was looking at her again.

"I don't want to walk the whole track, just one section. I thought, seeing as how you missed your second driving lesson, you could drive me out there."

"You want *me* to drive *you* on an F1 track?" The man was insane. The mystery of why he fancied her was solved.

"Not in Eva." He stroked his hand along the side pod of his F1 car. God, now she was jealous of a hunk of carbon fiber.

"You named your car?"

"We spend a lot of quality time together. What I meant was we'd use a regular car to drive out to the turn in question. Then I'll get out and walk."

"Um, I guess. There won't be other drivers

walking the track, will there?" She could see the headlines now: "Unlicensed woman mows down half of Formula 1's drivers."

"No, most of them have left the track now."

"All right, then. If you think it's safe."

"You're with me. What could go wrong?" For one, he could smile at her like that and she'd drive straight into a wall.

"Why do you insist on tempting fate by saying these things?"

"I don't believe in fate."

Until meeting Daniel, she hadn't either. But now it felt like her whole life had been leading up to this one experience.

He led her to a small compact car and handed her the keys. They were sitting so much closer than they had been in the Land Rover. She drew in a deep breath, filling her head with his scent. They'd be lucky to get to the end of the pit lane without crashing.

"Are you still angry with me about last night?" she asked before turning the key in the ignition.

"Anger is dangerous on the track. So I've come up with a plan. But you have to get me safely back to the garage before I'm going to tell you what it is."

"And if I don't?"

"Then I guess you'll never know." He winked then turned serious. "Now, first thing you need to do is find the bite point on the clutch. Keep the revs up a bit then slowly lift pressure from the clutch until you can feel the car start to rise. Then put the handbrake down and gently press the accelerator as you release the clutch."

She did as he instructed. The car leapt forward and then stalled. She tried it again and again until finally they moved off in a somewhat smooth motion, albeit slowly. He kept up the calm instructions, guiding her hand on the gear lever as she shifted into second and then third. Halfway around the track he had her stop and try the start again. This time she moved off on the first attempt, although her gear change would have made a mechanic cry. Finally, they arrived at the piece of track Daniel wanted to walk.

She stopped the car and they both got out. He walked the curve twice, often kneeling down to touch the surface. Then he almost lay on the curb as he studied the camber, using a marble. "There, that's the problem," he announced after about half an hour.

"What? I don't see anything."

He showed her a minor inconsistency in the surface. It couldn't be more than three millimeters' difference, but evidently it was enough to throw off the downforce on his car. He spent another ten minutes checking out the tarmac before heading back to the car. She expected him to take the driver's seat and get them back to the garages in record time. Instead he opened the passenger door and put on his seatbelt. She managed to pull away smoothly, and Daniel cheered as though she'd won a race.

"One more time around," he said as they neared the pit lane entrance. "This time, try to go a little faster and see if you can get into fourth or fifth gear."

They made two more laps of the track, going faster each time. By the time he called the lesson at an end and she successfully parked the car at the end of the pit lane, her heart rate was soaring and she felt she could take on the world. Daniel made her believe she could do anything. If only she'd met him five years ago.

"Thank you, Daniel. You don't know how much this means to me." She forced back the tears.

"Good. Then you'll agree to my plan. We're going to have dinner —just you and me. I know a place where we can talk without anyone overhearing. Best of all, no paparazzi."

He wanted to talk? Wasn't that supposed to be her line? "I'd like that. I'll let Genevieve know. You have a car?" At his nod she continued, "I'll meet you down in the parking garage then at seven."

Daniel didn't look thrilled at the meet location but agreed. "Bring a change of clothes."

Did she want to be taken to a dinner that required two outfits?

***

Lexy took his breath away when she arrived in the parking garage. How did the woman become more beautiful each time he saw her? Must be her blossoming confidence. He sensed that she'd faked it before, pretending a bravado that she didn't really feel. But now? Now it was genuine. She walked with purpose, her shoulders back, no longer holding her hands over her stomach and hunched forward as if trying to hide her figure. The black dress hugged her curves like an oil slick. *Dieu*, he'd better not crash and burn tonight. He couldn't take many more sleepless nights, tossing and turning, wishing she were there with him. With the race two days away, he needed to concentrate. Instead, his mind was full of Lexy as she'd been in the library before Max had called.

It wasn't the imminence of sex putting a huge smile on her face now, though. She doubled over in laughter and he caught a glimpse of a red lace bra. His body hardened.

"Oh, my God. I can't believe you're driving a Lada." Lexy jumped into the passenger seat, not waiting for him to come around and open the door. Any other woman he'd taken for dinner would have refused to get in such an ugly car. Lexy clearly didn't give a shit about money, or prestige, or appearances. What else did he have to offer her? Tonight wasn't for dark thoughts, though. Tonight was for finding a way forward that they could both live with. At least for the next seven weeks.

Pretending it was the greatest sports car ever, Daniel revved the engine. It stalled. "You wanted anonymity. This is the last car on earth anyone would expect me to drive."

"Reliability trumps anonymity. Do you think it will get us to our destination? Is it far?"

"It just has to get us six blocks to where the real car is parked." There, they transitioned into a dark blue Ferrari 488 GTB. "Now this is more like it," he said as he drove away from Sochi towards the mountains. He forced his eyes to remain on the tight, twisty road and off the extra ten centimeters of Lexy's leg exposed when she'd slid into the low-slung car. The Ferrari did handle great on the curves, but he'd rather be handling Lexy's.

The lights of the city were far beneath them when he pressed a button on the instrument panel and a set of iron gates swung open. He followed a long driveway steadily upwards until he parked in front of a huge villa. It looked like it had been picked up in Tuscany and dropped here by mistake.

"Where are we?" No trepidation, just curiosity.

"At my friend Sasha's place. This is his car. He's traveling at the moment but said we could have dinner here. He has a fantastic chef."

As he helped her from the car, the front door opened and a uniformed butler ushered them inside. Dinner was set up on the back terrace. The lights of Sochi twinkled below against the darkness of the Black Sea. But the best surprise he was saving for after dinner.

Lexy was still admiring the view when the butler returned with a silver platter and two glasses of sparkling wine. Daniel handed one to her but waved the other away. "I never drink from Thursday night until after the race on Sunday," he explained. He liked to keep his head clear. At the moment it was fogged with the scent of Lexy's perfume.

He couldn't remember anything he ate; his attention was absorbed by the woman across from him. But from the rapturous expression on Lexy's face, she enjoyed it. When the butler brought the dessert, however, she took one bite then pushed her plate away.

She also waved away a second glass of champagne and thanked the man in Russian. At least that's what he figured she said; his Russian had never progressed beyond thank you.

"Don't you like it?" he asked as Sasha's beaming staff member retreated to the kitchen.

"Too much. I've already put on a kilogram this week with all the delicious food."

"I can't tell."

"But I can." She turned her head and stared at the view.

"Do you worry about your weight?"

"I think I always will. It was really hard to break all the bad eating habits my mother forced upon me. When I'm stressed or sad, my first reaction is to eat. But I don't want to go back to what I was. Ever. However, I also have to make sure I don't go to the opposite extreme. For a while, every forkful of food I put in my mouth I asked myself, 'Do I need this or just want it?'"

"How did you handle your pregnancy? Was the weight gain difficult?"

"You know, you're the first person to ask me that. But yes, it was in a way. I forced myself to eat for Max's sake, but at every weigh-in I panicked that I was getting fat again. Food is always going to be an issue for me. But as long as I keep the rest of my life in balance, hopefully my weight will stay relatively constant. I'm working hard to maintain where I am now. I know I'll never be skinny, but I'm healthy."

"You're more than healthy. If you think it would

help, you could work out with me in the morning. I hate exercising, but I might not mind so much if you were there."

She smiled, and for some stupid reason his chest swelled and his fingers tingled. What the hell?

"I'd like that," she said.

He pulled in a deep breath, trying to calm his racing heart. "Speaking of exercise, want to go for a walk?"

"Here? It's pitch-black."

"The path is lit to what I want to show you."

"Oh, I love surprises."

He took her hand and led her to the end of the terrace and then along a narrow pathway until they arrived at a special room nestled against the hillside. Daniel unlocked the door with the key Sasha had told him about, and let Lexy precede him.

"Wow." She moved to the floor-to-ceiling window and stared at the view. All of Sochi was laid out before them. The lights of the Olympic park and the F1 circuit were easy to spot. She was so entranced by the view that she hadn't commented on the huge bed in the room. With the glass ceiling, it was the perfect place to view the stars in comfort. Or do other things. He was really hoping for other things. He came up behind her and wrapped his arms around her waist, inhaling deeply of her scent—a mix of shampoo, perfume, and non-distilled Lexy.

"Do you enjoy looking at the stars?" he asked, his lips on her ear. His tongue flicked across her lobe and she shivered.

"Of course, who doesn't? Although, we don't see many of them in London. Too much light pollution." Her last words came out with a low moan as his hands slipped up to cup her breasts, his thumbs tracing the outline of her nipples through her clothes.

"Come see the stars." He backed her up to the bed and waited for her to climb up. He wouldn't force her. Not even seduce her. She had to want this.

She sat on the bed, braced on her hands behind her, her head flung back as she checked out the glass ceiling. He bit down on his lip at the erotic image she projected. "Who the hell owns a secluded bedroom with a glass wall and ceiling? Not to mention the biggest bed I've ever seen."

He had to clear his throat before he could speak. "Sasha Kasparov. He plays in the NHL. If you want a real playboy for your next advertising campaign, he's your man. Doesn't even restrict himself to one woman a night, or at a time for that matter. But he's a huge F1 fan and lets me take advantage of his amazing house when we come to Russia."

"You've brought other women here?"

"No, you're the only one. I usually sleep here at least one night, alone, to get away from the mayhem down in the valley."

"So, you brought me here to look at the stars and sleep?" Her voice was flat.

Merde, he should have put the lights on so he could read her expression.

"Well, if there are other things you'd like to do, I'm open to suggestions."

"Come here, you daft man, and make love to me."

"Are you sure?" he asked, but he was already unbuttoning his shirt.

"You are officially the worst playboy ever. I'm going to have to give you lessons before the next advertising campaign begins."

He paused then blurted out, "I'm not really a playboy. It's all an act."

"What?" She flicked on the bedside lamp and stared at him, her brown eyes wanting to believe.

"Yep. You'll find me in bed with a book every night, not a different woman."

"But the photos … the press … the women…"

"Smoke and mirrors. When I want to leave somewhere or someone, I say I've got a blonde or brunette or redhead waiting for me. I just never go on to say they're the characters in the book I'm reading."

"But I've seen pictures of you leaving parties and events with women, never the same one twice."

He smiled. "I'm a gentleman. I see my dance partner, or plus one, back to her place, give her a kiss on the cheek, and leave. Then I let my supposed reputation do the rest. If you were a supermodel, would you want to be known as the one who couldn't get Daniel Michaud into bed? They're too embarrassed by my departure to ever say anything."

She laughed. A genuine, from the belly, laugh that bounced off the glass walls. "Are you serious?"

"Deadly."

"I'm finding this hard to believe. Fess up, when's the last time you had sex? And you have to be honest."

So, the gloves were off. It was rather refreshing to have a frank discussion and not have to wrap everything in political correctness.

"Eight months ago, about three months after Jacques and Grand-Papa left. It was pre-season so I didn't have my team around and I was lonely. I met a woman in a café in Paris. She was far from home and lonely, too." They'd both gotten what they wanted out of the hook-up—a night of not being alone. He hadn't heard from her again, couldn't even remember her full name. "What about you?"

"Three years, ten months, and six days ago."

Mon Dieu. "That's very precise." Was she kidding? She was a vibrant, sexy woman. What was the reason for her abstinence?

"That's because three years, ten months, and *four* days ago, my husband walked out the door. Evidently taking my sex life with him."

"*Merde*. And since then…"

"Nothing. I want this one night with you, Daniel. Not to get over a drought, but because you make me feel things no other man ever has. Now, are you done talking?" She turned off the lamp, bathing the room in moonlight.

"I'm done talking." He pulled off his shirt and reached for her. If they were only going to have this one night, it damned well was going to be spectacular.

He kissed her. He may not be a genuine playboy, but he didn't need advice. Just to taste her, feel her silky skin, and hear the sound of her enjoyment.

When he released her lips she pushed away from

him and moved to the middle of the room, where she slithered out of her dress. He swallowed at the sight of her red lacy lingerie against the paleness of her skin in the moonlight. Soon even those scraps of fabric fell to the floor, and he was mesmerized as she sauntered over to where he still sat on bed.

"You're falling behind. Need a hand?"

"Yes," he managed to get out seconds before she pushed him onto his back and straddled him. After that his mind went blank as she removed his clothes, her hands and lips caressing and teasing him until all he could hear was his blood pounding in his ears. If he didn't want to have an aneurysm, he had to get back in control.

"My turn." He flipped her over so he was on top. He wanted the connection to last long after they left the bed. He wanted Lexy to forget everything but him and how they made each other feel.

"Now, Daniel. Get inside me now," she begged as her head thrashed from side to side. He was bringing her close to the edge then retreating, desperate to prolong this moment as long as possible.

"Not yet," he said more to himself than her.

"Box, box, box," she screamed as an orgasm ripped through her. The command to come into the pits for a tire change took on a whole new meaning. She grabbed his head, pulling his mouth from where he'd been pleasuring her.

He slid immediately into her heat, thankful he'd put a condom on earlier. With a passion-filled laugh she wrapped her legs around his ribs, and he followed her into a vortex of pleasure. As they lay side by side several minutes later, staring at the stars, Lexy's husky voice filled the room. "Damn, Daniel. That was amazing."

Amazing was an understatement. He had enough experience to know when the sex was phenomenal. The connection he'd felt that first night in the library had been magnified tenfold. He hauled in an unsteady breath. "Are you sure one night is all you want?"

"What I want is to do that again. When you're ready."

His cock stirred to life at her words. As she rolled on top of him and flicked her tongue on his nipples, a meteor streaked through the sky above them.

His need to not lose focus was soon incinerated in the heat of their passion. Had he just killed his championship hopes?

Chapter Ten

Lexy paced, wishing she'd worn flat shoes. At least she was burning off the calories from last night's dinner. Although she'd probably have already done that with the two rounds of lovemaking with Daniel. He certainly wasn't the type of man to climb on top, lift up her night shirt, and jiggle it about for two minutes before collapsing on top of her. No, he wasn't satisfied until he'd wrung every ounce of pleasure from the moment, until she begged him to fill her.

Now said man was hurtling around the track with nineteen other cars, each trying to out-accelerate and out-brake the other. And this was only qualifying. She'd be a complete mess during the race tomorrow if she didn't find something to distract her. A lock of hair slid across her face, surprising her with its softness. There was a lot to be said for a £200 cut and blow dry. Even more fun had been the girl-talk with Mandy, Louisa, and Tara. Although they were beautiful, wealthy women for whom dropping a couple hundred on a haircut wasn't a problem, they were still down to earth and dedicated to the men they loved.

"And that's session one done," the TV announcer said. "The only surprise elimination is one of the Ferraris. Get ready for round two. We'll be back on track in ten minutes."

Three rounds of qualifying determined grid position for tomorrow's race. The five slowest cars were dropped in the first session, then the next five slowest, until in the final round the top ten cars battled it out for pole position. To be first on the grid was an advantage every one of the drivers coveted. Daniel wasn't the fastest man on the track at this point. But it was the final session that mattered. The fact that he hadn't had to use the quicker tire at this stage gave him another advantage for the race tomorrow.

Lexy unclenched her hands and tried to sit until the next session began. She was too nervous to be in Daniel's garage, and she didn't want to distract him when he needed his entire focus on the track. So she'd retreated to his trailer to watch the proceedings on the monitor. The other reason she was hiding out here was she'd spotted her father wandering down the pit lane just before qualifying began. He looked so much older. And surprisingly enough, he didn't have a woman on his arm. Was he going through another divorce? After her mother, not one of his marriages had lasted more than two years.

The pit lane was also swarming with media from every country with an F1 fan base. So far she'd managed to stay hidden. But if her father saw her and threw a wobbly, she could pretty much guarantee the paparazzi would be all over it. With the next race in Texas, the very last thing she needed was for her picture to be splashed all over the internet. She couldn't avoid her father for long, however. She'd need some way to contact him discreetly so they could have their reunion in private. After qualifying, she'd find out which hotel he was staying at and then arrange to meet.

The advertising break was over and the two announcers were analyzing the performance of the cars from the first session. They noticed the different line that Daniel took around turn eight and commented on his innate feel for the track. Nothing innate about it, she wanted to yell at the TV. It was his dedication that made him examine every inch of track. A trait he also carried over to his lovemaking. There wasn't an inch of her body he hadn't touched or kissed. Her face grew hot just remembering.

"Knock, knock," a female voice called out. For God's sake, why didn't the person just knock? Probably didn't want to risk damaging a perfect manicure. If it was one of the grid girls hoping for a hook-up with Daniel later, Lexy'd set her straight. Although, what right did she have to do that? They'd had their one night.

Instead, standing at the door was Jacqueline Lefebre. From her position a few feet above Jacqueline's head, Lexy could see that all was not great in the other woman's world. She really wanted to be alone to watch the rest of qualifying. But Jacqueline was Daniel's friend, so she invited her in.

"So, you are the Lexy I have heard so much about." The woman's French accent was thick, unlike Daniel's. Should she offer to converse in French? Or keep the discussion in English and thus to her advantage?

"You must be Jacqueline. I'm afraid Daniel hasn't

been as forthcoming in information."

"Typical Daniel. He is so loyal. I wonder what I would do without him."

It was what she was doing with him that interested Lexy. How many calories were in fingernails? She just may take up Tara's habit after all.

"You're not watching the qualifying?" Lexy turned the telly down but not off. The second session was due to begin in five minutes and she hoped this visit would be over by then.

"It only gets interesting in Q3. And I wanted to meet you without Daniel around," Jacqueline said. She ran a shaking hand through her hair. Several strands fluttered to the floor. Lexy looked closer. Jacqueline's skin was gray and stretched tight across her cheeks, and not from filler injections. Her eyes were dull and slow to react to the darker interior inside the trailer. This woman was not healthy.

"Would you like to sit down? Can I get you a cup of tea or coffee?"

"I will sit, but I do not need a drink, thank you. I just came to introduce myself. It seems we have a lot in common."

"Oh?" Lexy leaned against the chair but didn't sit, needing the height advantage to give her confidence.

"Yes, we both love Daniel Michaud."

Lexy let the words hang between them, not quite sure how to respond. She could deny it, but she doubted she could say it convincingly enough for the other woman to believe her. A catfight hadn't been on her agenda for today, but she wasn't ruling it out.

"Are you here to tell me to stay away from Daniel?"

"Feisty. I see what Daniel likes about you."

"Why are you here, Jacqueline? If it's just a social visit, perhaps we can put it off until the reception tonight. I'd really like to watch the qualifying." And it would give her a chance to mentally prepare for this.

"I have come to explain that photo in the papers after Japan. I know Daniel will not. But he says I can trust you."

Lexy swallowed, not sure she wanted to know now. "You have my word."

Jacqueline stared at her chipped manicure. "I am a drug addict. With my husband's position as F1 doctor, if the general population knew, he would have to resign. Everyone will assume I get my drugs through him. I had been clean for almost six months, but I relapsed in Japan, in Daniel's room. I overdosed in his bathroom and passed out. He must have found me after he started to undress for bed. He was carrying me to my hotel room where my husband could take care of me when the photo was taken."

And why Daniel said it wasn't his secret to share. Lexy sank into the chair opposite Jacqueline. "Are you getting help?"

"Yes. It is just so *difficile*."

"I understand. My mother has an addiction to food. But she won't get help. I promise to keep your secret. Thank you for telling me, Jacqueline. I know it took a lot of courage for you to talk to me."

"Just be good to Daniel. He is special."

"I know."

"Daniel Michaud spins in turn twelve—" The announcer's excited voice swung Lexy's attention back to the TV.

"Oh, God," Lexy said, her eyes glued to the screen until she saw Daniel's car returning to the pits on the monitor. The announcer resumed his calm delivery of the events happening just outside her door. "That's that lap ruined and probably those tires as well. Will he have enough sets for tomorrow's race?" The rest of the commentary droned on, and she turned back to Jacqueline.

The other woman had left already.

***

Daniel got pole position by two hundredths of a second over his teammate. The difference came down to the time he gained by taking the alternate line at turn eight. Lexy sat in his trailer, stopping herself twice from going to the garage to congratulate him. She knew the international media would be hounding him and she wasn't practiced enough in hiding her emotions to fool anyone. One look at her and everyone would know she'd had sex with Daniel. If she got called back to London now, she'd forever regret not getting to spend the next seven weeks with him, even if it was just as a colleague.

So she sent Daniel a text telling him she was waiting in his trailer. She waited. And waited. Maybe he'd not seen her message and gone back to the hotel.

Her phone buzzed with an incoming text and she rushed to read it.

"Just spoke with your father. Are you ready to meet him? I can suggest he comes to the trailer so you can have your reunion in private."

Was she ready? "Yes, okay," she texted back.

Her stomach roiled and she gulped down a glass of water to quell the nausea. The trailer door flew open—*no, no, no. This is a bad idea*—but only Daniel appeared. His cocky grin sent her heart into overdrive. God, he was gorgeous.

"Congratulations on pole," she managed seconds before he swept her into a tight hug, lifted her off the floor, and swung her around, and then kissed her until she nearly blacked out.

"I've made a terrible mistake," Daniel said as he finally set her on her feet. She could feel the adrenaline still pumping through his veins in the tightness with which he held her and the hardness of his kiss.

"What's that?" From where she was, everything was going swimmingly.

"I should have told your father to meet me here in an hour rather than five minutes. That way we could properly celebrate my pole position."

"Rookie mistake," she acknowledged as his lips descended once more.

Five minutes flew by when you were playing tongue tag with an F1 driver. A knock on the door sprung them apart. Lexy straightened her top and smoothed her hair.

"Did you tell him I'm here?" she whispered as

Daniel shrugged off the shoulders of his overalls and tied the arms around his waist to hide his erection.

"No. He thinks I want to talk to him about the possibility of driving for Ferrari."

There was another knock on the door, this one more impatient. Her father had never been a man who liked to be kept waiting.

Daniel ran a hand down her bare arm then opened the door. Gian-Franco's gruff voice boomed through the enclosed space. "You ask me to come see you and then keep me waiting?"

This was not going to go well if her father was already angry. They'd just pick up exactly from where they parted ten years ago.

"Sorry, sir. But I'm sure when you see who's here to meet you, you'll forgive me."

"Who is it?" Before Daniel could answer, her father pushed his way into the trailer and stood, hands on his hips, staring at her. His eyes widened, his mouth flopped open, and all the color drained from his face. Oh God, was he having a heart attack? Had she just killed her father?

"Papa!" Lexy raced forward and grabbed her father's wrist to check his pulse. Her touch seemed to bring him back to his senses.

Color flushed back into his face as he turned angry eyes on Daniel. "You think hooking up with my daughter is going to get you a drive with Ferrari?"

"I don't need a woman to get a drive." Daniel's tone could have cooled the brakes on his car. "My work on the track does that."

"Then this meeting is over," Papa said before storming out of the trailer.

Lexy stared at the door, unaware tears were spilling down her face until Daniel wiped one away.

"I'm sorry," he murmured against her temple. "I had no idea he would react like that."

It would be so easy to sink into his embrace, let him take away her pain. But she needed to handle this herself. If she became reliant on him, where would she be in two months? Calling up the strong woman who had sat beside her son's NICU bed, she pulled out of Daniel's arms and scrubbed the wetness from her cheeks with the heels of her hands.

"It's fine. I'd better get back to the hotel. Max will be waking from his nap soon."

"Lexy…" Daniel tried to pull her back against him.

"No." She wrapped her arms around her torso. "Look, Daniel, my father has disappointed me all my life. I'm not sure why I expected it to be different this time. You may be my lover, if a one-night stand even qualifies for that title. But that's where it ends. You don't need to hold my hand or make things better for me."

"And that's where you're wrong. There is way more going on between us than one night of sex. And if you're not willing to admit that, then you're not the woman I thought you were."

Her eyes searched his. "I can't deal with this now. I have to go."

His trailer door slammed for the second time in ten minutes.

***

Daniel rinsed the shampoo from his hair in the shower. All his excitement at having taken pole position died when Lexy had said he was nothing more to her than a good lay. It was bad enough that he'd spun out on a corner when his chief mechanic had told him to "box" at the end of the lap. Remembering Lexy's command had distracted him for a split second and he'd put a wheel on the grass. If that happened during the race tomorrow…

It was exactly what he'd feared if he let a woman close during the race season. But for the life of him he couldn't break it off. Not yet. Tomorrow he'd force himself to concentrate on nothing but the tarmac in front of him and the cars behind. He'd done it last year as his life fell apart—first with Jacqueline's addiction spiraling out of control, and then his brother and pseudo- grandfather disappearing off the face of the earth. But it had taken its toll. He'd come in second in the championship. This was his year.

Or it had been. Until Lexy showed up. So now he needed a better plan. Sleeping with her once hadn't worked—it only made the longings worse. He'd convince her that they could have an affair until the end of the season. Having more of her would be less of a distraction than not having her at all. He'd win the championship with a grin on his face, she'd get her bonus and go back to psychology school, and everyone would be happy. Maybe he'd even keep in touch with Max and take him to some cart races or something, give him a tour of the team HQ. The kid would love that.

Daniel finished his shower, dressed, and was standing outside Lexy's hotel room door before he'd figured out what to say. He just knew he had to sort things out with her before he went to a reception in a nearby hotel. At least he wouldn't have to stay long, as he had the excuse of resting up for the race tomorrow. And Lexy had already arranged for him to be seen leaving with a woman—the sister of another driver's wife. Evidently she was a struggling actress and could use the publicity of a rumored affair with him. It sat like a bad taste in his mouth.

"Daniel." There was genuine relief in her voice.

"What's up?" He wanted to take her in his arms but daren't, even though Max was nowhere to be seen.

"My father just called. He's on his way up. He apologized for his reaction this afternoon and wants to talk. Do I look okay?" She smoothed her hand down a pale blue dress, one he hadn't seen before. It had a high neck and the hem fell an inch below her knees. It was fitted to the waist and then flared out over her hips. It was demure, practical, and pretty. Undoubtedly chosen with her father in mind. She'd also done something to her hair and now it fell in a smooth cascade of silk to the middle of her back, caressing her shoulders as she turned. He'd noticed it in the trailer but had been too impatient to kiss her to comment on the change.

"You look beautiful, as always. I like what you've done to your hair." He reached out and snagged one of the strands, letting the silky tresses slide through his fingers. It was impossibly soft.

"Thank you. I mean, do I look okay to see my father?"

"You saw him this afternoon, Lexy. What's up? Are you sure about seeing him again?"

She waved her hands in the air as if they would express her feelings. Sometimes, like now, she was pure Italian. "I have to give him another chance. He's my father."

"What about me?"

"What about you?" Her eyes turned wary.

"Do I get another chance with you? One night wasn't enough for me."

Her gaze shifted to the door, avoiding his. "It was for me."

"Liar." He took a step closer and ran a finger down the side of her face and over her lips, which quivered under his touch.

"Has Max's epical bad timing rubbed off on you? My father will be here any second."

"And there's a door between me and him. I want an answer. Do I get another chance with you?"

His lips were inches from hers, but he refused to bridge the distance until she answered. Her sigh was part wistful, part resignation. "Possibly. Tomorrow, after the race—we can discuss it then."

He feathered kisses from her mouth to her ear. "I hope *discuss* is a euphemism."

Before she could reply, Max came hurtling into the room and Daniel scooped him up, reluctantly releasing Lexy. "My mummy says a man is coming and all he says is 'no,'" Max said, wrapping his chubby arms around Daniel's neck as though seeking protection.

Lexy gave a nervous laugh. "I made the mistake of telling Max that his grandfather is Italian, so he should call him *nonno.*"

Daniel nodded. "Once he sees you, Max, your *nonno* will be saying '*Si, si.*'"

"C?" Max asked. "Is that his favorite letter? Mine is Z because it looks the tracks of a car going really fast. Or maybe S. I like M, too, because that's for both Max and Mummy…"

Lexy shook her head. "I am so regretting not teaching him some Italian."

There was a knock and Max's little arms tightened even more. Forget falling off the track for thinking of Lexy—Daniel might not make it to the race tomorrow because he'd been strangled by a three-year-old.

"Max, go in the other room with Genevieve, please," Lexy whispered.

Daniel put the little boy down, who then raced into the bedroom. "Do you want me to leave as well?"

"No, actually, I'd like you to stay." She gave him a hesitant smile then wiped her hands down her dress again before stepping around him to answer the door.

Gian-Franco raised an eyebrow when he saw Daniel but made no comment.

"Papa, didn't you have something you wanted to say to Daniel?" Lexy prompted.

"I apologize for my behavior earlier," Gian-Franco said. "I already had two young men try to bribe me this weekend to get a test drive with Ferrari. And my wife, she filed for divorce yesterday. I was not in a good mind, and seeing my daughter with you, I jumped to conclusions. You are an excellent driver, Daniel. Ferrari would be lucky to have you."

"Thank you, but I'm quite happy with my current team."

"I'm sorry to hear about your marriage," Lexy said, leading the way to the sitting room.

"Some men are not meant to be married. I guess I'm one of them. I had thought you were the same, Daniel. What are your intentions toward my daughter?"

He should have left when he'd had the chance. Because he was fairly certain "bang her until the race season is done then get on with my life" wasn't the kind of thing you said to a girl's father. Even if the girl and father hadn't seen each other in ten years.

"Papa, that's none of your business. But for the record, Daniel and I are colleagues." Lexy went on to explain about her job and the Destin Designs contract, leaving out any mention of Jacqueline. Gian-Franco didn't look convinced that was the full extent of Daniel's relationship with his daughter, but he let it pass.

Gian-Franco took Lexy's hand in his own. "And your mother? How is she?" There was a hint of nostalgia in his voice.

"She's still the same. She can't get out of bed anymore and has a home care assistant clean her and prepare her meals. I've done all I can. Until she wants help, it's better if I stay away."

"I'm glad you're okay."

"Papa, those things I said—"

"Are forgiven long ago. I'm sorry I didn't come back to try again to take you away. I was so angry that your mother had done that to you. But I could understand you not wanting to leave her when you were all she had."

"I needed to find my own way out. To get the strength from within."

Daniel sat back and let the drama of father-daughter reunion play out in front of him.

That afternoon he'd received another message from his alleged half brother asking Daniel to meet his purported father after the race in Rio. He hadn't dismissed the request as quickly as he had in the past. Instead, he'd Googled Santiago Alvarez and discovered that the man was very wealthy in his own right. So it was unlikely that he'd be asking Daniel for money. Still, there had to be a catch, didn't there? Why bother after all these years?

But if Daniel had a child … if Lexy conceived and then didn't tell him about it and years later he found out… He struggled to pull in a breath. He'd move heaven and earth to see his son or daughter. Could he expect less of another man? It wasn't going to cost him anything except time to find out if this person was really his father.

Lexy had given her father a second chance. Maybe it was time he gave his father a first one. Heaven knew his mother was no paragon of virtue. What if she'd been the one to hide Daniel's conception and birth from the man? His mother was all about the money; if this man hadn't any at the time, she probably had never bothered to contact him.

"Papa, can you keep a secret?" Lexy's question brought Daniel back from his own parental issues. She wasn't about to tell Gian-Franco they were lovers, was she? His heart rate sped up. Gian-Franco nodded but scowled at Daniel. He knew the other man hadn't believed the "we're colleagues" gambit.

"I have a son, but no one outside of this room can know he exists," Lexy said.

"Is he the father?" Gian-Franco glared at him.

"No, it's not Daniel. It's someone else. We were married very briefly. Papa, if you want to meet Max, you have to keep absolutely quiet about his existence."

"You expect me not to tell the world that I have a grandson? What's going on here, Alexandra?"

She stared at the carpet. From shame? The hesitation was back in her voice when she told her father the story of her brief marriage. Something wasn't right here, but damned if Daniel could figure it out.

"I won't say anything," Gian-Franco finally agreed. Lexy went to get Max, probably to give herself a minute, as she could have easily called out for him.

"Here," Daniel said, pulling a tiny toy Ferrari from his pocket and handing it to Gian-Franco. "Max is car-crazy. I was going to give him this, but he'd probably like it better from his grandfather."

Max came into the room, clutching Lexy's hand. Daniel had never seen him so sedate. Gian-Franco looked like he was about to burst into tears.

"I'm so happy to meet you, *mio nipote*."

"My name is Max."

Both Lexy and Gian-Franco burst into happy tears. Max looked at Daniel as if to say, "Are we the only non-crazies here?"

Given the emotion welling in his own throat, Daniel wasn't so sure where he stood on the side of sanity. All he knew was that he'd better get away before he was sucked in any deeper.

Chapter Eleven

He won! As he sprayed the champagne at the crowd, his eyes searched for Lexy. She hadn't shown at the party last night, and then this morning had texted him that she was going to watch the race from the Ferrari garage with her father. But surely she should be below with the throng of fans watching the trophy presentation. Daniel gritted his teeth.

"Where's your bird?" Robert, his teammate and second-place finisher in today's race asked as he poured the remainder of his champagne over Daniel's head.

"Lexy? Not sure. And you know…"

"Yeah, yeah, my wife told me. Secret love affair. Good luck with that, mate. With this crowd watching your every move, you haven't got a hope in hell of keeping it off the media radar."

He didn't think so either. And at the moment, he wasn't even sure they had an affair to keep secret. He hadn't had a chance to talk to her about extending their one-night stand into a two-month fling.

Three grid girls paraded out in their high heels and handed each of the drivers a microphone. The woman who handed one to him also passed her phone number. He surreptitiously dropped the paper and forced his media smile, all the while wondering where Lexy was.

He answered the routine questions: "How does it feel to win?" "Great." "Do you think you can do it again in Texas?" "Hope so." "What about the championship?" "Ask me after Abu Dhabi…" When asked how he was going to celebrate tonight he managed not to say, "Ideally, by having repeated off-the-charts sex with the woman I can't find at the moment." Instead he said something about a bubble bath that made the crowd laugh.

Lexy wasn't waiting in his garage either. Or his trailer. By the time everything was squared away and he could leave the track, his jaw ached from grinding his teeth. There was no message on his phone and she wasn't in either his hotel room or hers, although Genevieve was there with Max and Lexy's father. All they could tell him was that she'd come straight back after the race, grabbed her dress, and disappeared again.

What the hell was going on? He showered off the champagne and dressed in what Destin Designs called a casual suit for the victory party. Casual and suit usually didn't go together, but it was comfortable while still looking classy. When Lexy still hadn't shown after thirty minutes, he thought about going to the front desk to have her paged.

Alexandra Camparelli, please join the race winner before he goes insane.

Instead he downed his second drink and went to get another one.

He almost dropped his glass when she arrived. If it hadn't been for the dress, which looked as amazing on her as he'd expected, he would have passed her by as another F1 hanger-on. She'd added a subtle red color to her hair, her makeup was dark and dramatic, and she walked like she could have any man in the room and knew it. Several male glances followed her progress across to him. His palm hurt and he looked down to see his hand was clenched so tightly he'd left nail prints.

The slight tremble in her hand as she put it on his arm, before she stood on her tiptoes and whispered "congratulations" into his ear, was the only sign of nerves. If she'd been taking WAG lessons, she'd aced it.

He put his empty glass down on the nearest level surface and directed her out onto the terrace. The beat of the music was muted and the light level so low he could barely see her eyes.

"I meant to be here earlier but—"

The rest of her excuse was swallowed by his kiss. He ravaged her lips, demanding her surrender. There was no gentleness in his touch, just pure hunger. He swiveled so her back was against the wall. He pulled her leg up and anchored it around his waist then slid his hand under to access her core. *Dieu*, she was commando. She was already wet and bucked against his thigh as he found her most sensitive spot. He released her lips to trail kisses across her jaw and down under her ear to her neck.

"If I'd known this was the reaction I'd get, I'd have gotten glammed up sooner," she whispered. Her voice was husky with desire, her breath coming in quick, sharp pants.

"No." He nipped along her collarbone, intoxicated

by her scent. "Don't get me wrong, you're beautiful. But I prefer the real Lexy. The one with slightly frizzy hair and natural makeup and eyes that make me want to kiss you until they glaze over with desire."

"Trust me, they're glazed. So if this isn't about my new look, why have you gone all caveman on me? Not that I'm complaining."

He raised his head long enough to take in the picture she presented. Her hair had come loose from half its pins and hung in chunks around her shoulders. Her lipstick was smeared and her lips swollen. And now that his pupils had had time to adjust, he could indeed see that her eyes had the glazed look of a woman caught in the throes of passion. This was how he wanted her.

While he could watch her face, he found her most sensitive spot and rubbed it. She quivered in her arms and bit down on her bottom lip. "I'm claiming my prize. If you didn't notice, I won the race today."

She released the zipper on his trousers and slid a finger inside. Space was tight, seeing as how he had an erection harder than the Eiffel Tower.

"I'm the victor's spoils, am I? What if Robert had won, or Mika, or Stephano?"

"They have to get their own spoils. You're mine."

Enough talking. He took her lips again in a blistering kiss. He moved the hand that wasn't pleasuring her to cup her breast, rubbing his thumb over her nipple through the fabric of her dress.

Lights exploded behind his eyelids. *Dieu*, he hadn't even come and already he was seeing stars. The flashes, however, were accompanied by the *click* of a camera shutter. *Merde*. He'd forgotten they were in a public place. He withdrew his hand and placed her leg back down on the ground. He zipped up his fly and dragged in a deep breath. It did little to clear the lust fog from his brain.

"Keep your head in my neck," he whispered into her ear, his voice harsher than he meant it to be. "I don't think they can see your face."

He turned his head to stare at the photographer. "Show's over. Get the hell out of my party."

Seconds later two burly security guards escorted the photographer off the terrace. As soon as they were gone, Daniel kept his arm wrapped tightly around Lexy as she walked with her head down, her hair shielding her face. Inside, the celebration was in full swing and most of the partygoers were well on their way to shit-faced. No one paid any attention to them as they skirted the edge of the room and through the employees-only door. He led her to the service elevator and then punched the button for her floor.

Lexy hadn't said a word yet, but from the tight way she held herself, she was either angry or scared. As soon as the elevator doors closed he lifted her face with a finger under her chin.

"Lexy? Are you okay?"

Her eyes were panicked, her gaze darting about the elevator, skipping over his face. "Oh God, this is exactly what I thought would happen if I got together with you. Mr. Petersen is going to fire me, I'll have to pay back the twenty grand, which I don't have, Wesley is going to see my photo and discover I have his child and sue me for custody and win…" Her voice got higher as she recounted each potential disaster.

"None of that is going to happen. The photographer didn't even see your face." He put a hand on her cheek, but she pushed him away.

"No, but someone will tell him who I am. My whole life ruined over one moment of stupidity."

"Lexy, calm down. It'll all be fine. By the end of the night, that photographer will have a dozen equally scandalous pictures. He's going to choose the one where he can see both faces. And even if he does choose ours, all he's got is me romancing a ravishing brunette. Your boss will be ecstatic; he'll have no idea it's you."

She slumped into the corner of the elevator. "Easy for you to say. What do you know about struggling to keep it together? You've had it all from birth."

He ignored the sting of her accusations. "I may not have had your financial struggles, but I do know what it's like to want something so badly and see it slip from your fingers. Don't let this one hiccup ruin what we have together." He put a hand on her shoulder, and when she didn't resist he slowly pulled her into his arms.

"What do we have together, Daniel?" Her deep sigh slid down the open neck of his shirt.

"Passion, friendship, a mutual love of reading…" *An intangible something that keeps me thinking of you long after we've parted and makes me reach for you in the middle of the night.*

"And that's worth risking my son for?"

He raised her face so she could see how serious he was. "If I thought for one second that being with me would jeopardize your custody of Max, I'd walk away from you right now."

"You would?"

"*Absolument.* I would never do anything to hurt you or your son."

Her eyes searched his. "I believe you. Sorry I overreacted. You should be celebrating. That was an amazing drive today."

"I'm exactly where I want to be. With you."

She pulled his head down as though to kiss him when the elevator doors *binged* as they opened. Getting caught in another compromising embrace would definitely kill any chance he had of convincing Lexy they could continue sleeping together. Daniel stuck his head out to make sure the coast was clear then escorted Lexy to her room. The night of passion he'd anticipated since he parked his car in front of the big number one now seemed a distant fantasy.

Lexy turned to him as she unlocked her door. The room was dark inside. "My father took Max and Genevieve out to dinner. Come in for a minute?" At least she hadn't shut the door in his face.

She moved across the room, picked up the room service menu, and started flipping through the pages.

"You haven't eaten?" He'd snacked at the buffet while waiting for her.

She gripped the folder tighter. "I ate with Mandy and Louisa while I was getting ready."

He put a hand on the menu. “Then do you really want this?”

“No. It’s just a stress reflex.” She tossed it onto the sofa.

He removed a couple of pins that stuck out of her hair and the rest of the silky strands tumbled down. “Anything I can do to make you feel less stressed?”

She tilted her head to one side and stared at him for a long moment. Finally, a sexy smile curved her lips. “Well, if you’re offering. A little more of what you started earlier would probably relax me.”

“*Cherie*, if that relaxed you, I’m doing it all wrong.”

“Then you’d better do it till you get it right. But in my room. I’m done with being interrupted.” Taking his hand, she led him to her bedroom.

Before he could offer to help, she undid the zipper at the back of her dress and let it fall to the floor. She stood there naked, except for a pair of killer stilettos. Her smile as she advanced on him was equally as wicked. “Now, where were we?”

Way beyond the point of no return.

***

Lexy woke to the sound of her bedroom door opening. Was Daniel sneaking out before they were caught? No, he was spooned against her back, one possessive arm anchoring her to him, his breath ruffling the top of her hair. Maybe she’d imagined the noise. It wouldn’t surprise her if her hearing was off; he’d blown quite a few of her circuits last night. It had been a no-holds-barred, every fantasy explored night of passion. When they'd heard Max and Genevieve return they'd gone into stealth mode, each trying to make the other break the silence. Thankfully, she knew that once Max was asleep, a tornado blowing through the room wouldn't wake him. And if Genevieve heard … well, she was a big girl.

A small hand touched her face.

So busted.

"Mummy, did Daniel have a bad dream?"

Daniel tensed behind her, obviously woken by Max's voice, at its usual loud volume.

"What?" Daniel asked.

"I'm only allowed to sleep in Mummy's bed if I have a bad dream," Max explained.

"Yes, I did have a bad dream. And your mummy was very good at soothing me so I could sleep again."

She resisted a snort. They'd fallen asleep at six a.m., and, glancing at the clock, it was barely eight now.

"Max, do you think you could wait for Genevieve to get up and then go down to the restaurant for breakfast? I have a headache and need a bit more sleep," Lexy said.

"Yep. Vivi said I could have chocolate pancakes with bananas." With that announcement he skipped out of the room, slamming the door behind him.

"First a photographer, now a three-year-old. We suck at this discretion thing," Daniel said, his lips on her shoulder. "Why can't we just come clean?"

"There's too much at stake—my job and Max's father. I don't want to risk that on a holiday affair."

He sat up in the bed, his morning stubble, bed hair, and sleepy eyes reawakening the sex addict inside her again. Except there was anger in his eyes, not passion.

"What if I want more than a holiday affair?" The question seemed to startle him as well, but he didn't take it back.

"I think you don't know what you want. You've never had a relationship last longer than a race."

"So you should realize how special you are to me."

"More likely I'm a novelty. Once the excitement wears off, you'll realize I'm pretty boring and you'll move on to someone new." Damn, that even hurt to say. But she'd managed it without a waver in her voice. *Now, if I can just hold back the tears until I hit the shower.*

Daniel leapt from the bed.

"I'm not a player. I thought you knew me by now."

God, this was not how she wanted today to go. They had a long, long flight to Texas. If he was angry with her, it would be unbearable. But she wasn't one to hide from the truth. She was a novelty, different from the women he normally associated with. She knew that. Soon he would, too.

"Daniel, don't leave angry," she said as he pulled on his trousers. "Come back to bed, or we can go for breakfast with Max and Genevieve."

He continued to dress, not looking at her. "No. I need to be alone for a while. I'll meet you here at your suite at ten tonight and we'll go to the airport together.

That is, of course, if you're willing to risk being seen with me under the cover of darkness."

"For God's sake, Daniel, you're behaving like Max." She sat up but kept the sheet clutched to her naked chest. Without his body heat, the bed already felt cold.

"Well, you know what they say about men, we're just boys with bigger toys."

He tugged on his shoes and then left. She heard him talking to Max for a minute before the door to the hallway shut behind him.

That had not been part of the script. She checked her phone. Another message of congratulations from her boss on Daniel being caught literally with his hands full last night. He reminded her of the fifty grand bonus if she kept Daniel on the straight and narrow, or, in this case, the wild and horny. As Daniel had predicted, Mr. Petersen had no idea the woman in the photo was her. He was probably still of the opinion that Alexandra Camparelli couldn't attract a man like Daniel Michaud. Well, she'd proven him wrong. Attracting hadn't been an issue. If only she had a reasonable shot at holding on to him. But hadn't her mother always told her not to get too attached to an attractive man? And they didn't come better-looking than Daniel.

Later that afternoon, when Max had his nap, Lexy tried to lie down as well. But she couldn't sleep. She looked at the internet photos of her and Daniel. Her hair had obscured her face, but other bits of her were definitely showing. Thankfully, the rest of the partygoers had held the line and not divulged her name.

So she'd simply been dubbed conquest number twenty-six. It sickened her that someone was keeping tabs.

The image of her mother's face when they'd walked in on her father having sex all those decades ago flashed into her mind. Would that be Lexy in a few years if she stayed with Daniel, if that was even an option? Would she end up like her mother, heartbroken, with no desire to carry on?

You'll never keep a good-looking man.

No, this thing with Daniel was an affair; there was no future in it. After Abu Dhabi, they'd part. She only hoped that maybe they could stay friends.

Yeah, right. She wasn't capable of that much detachment.

By the time Daniel knocked on the door at ten p.m., her anxiety level was at DEFCON 1. Wesley was going to find them and take Max away. Daniel was going to realize she was just a boring woman with a kid and move on. And Lexy would systematically eat her way through the entire Ben & Jerry's ice cream collection.

Max was making a valiant effort to stay awake, clutching Dude's bowl, which nearly slid from his grasp twice. Lexy took the fish away and Max began to howl. *God, I can't even get this right.*

"Here, let me," Daniel said. He scooped Max up with one arm and relieved her of the fishbowl with the other hand. Genevieve was busy making sure they hadn't left any of Max's toys. They'd arrived with three bags and were leaving with seven, thanks mostly to her father, who felt he had to make up for every missed

Christmas and birthday in one go. If this rate of accumulation continued for the entire trip, they'd need a jumbo jet to get them home.

"Genevieve, did you get Max's asthma inhaler from the bedside table?" Lexy asked as her gaze did one last sweep of the room. She'd forgotten something, she knew it. Probably her mind.

"Got it," Genevieve confirmed.

Somehow they managed to get to the airport, through immigration, and onto the plane without mishap. Max was asleep before the landing gear was up, and Genevieve's eyes were closed, her seat fully reclined.

"There's a bed through that door." Daniel inclined his head toward the rear of the plane. "You'll be more comfortable in there."

"You take it—you're taller. You won't get an ounce of sleep in these chairs."

"Lexy…" He glanced at Genevieve and then closed his mouth.

Lexy stood, held out her hand, and went with him into the bedroom. As soon as the door was closed, however, he dropped her hand and stood by the door.

"Daniel, this morning … this thing with you"—she waved her hand in the air as though the words were somewhere in the vicinity and she could knock them into her mouth—"it's way more intense than I ever imagined. However, as fantastic as it is and as crazy as I am about you I can't see a future for us. I don't want to end up like my mother."

He sat next to her on the bed and put an arm

around her shoulders. "I wasn't expecting this either. I thought we could just have some fun between the sheets while we're together. But somewhere along the line it's become more than that to me. What more, I don't know. Give us time, Lexy, to figure this out together. Don't retire from the race until we've exhausted all the options."

"I should never have entered the race in the first place. For God's sake, I don't even drive." She should have ignored the chemistry between them and just done her job. Now she was in danger of exchanging a food addiction for a Daniel obsession.

"We can't go back to just colleagues now. Not after what we've shared. Let's take this thing to the end."

The end of my sanity?

"What do you mean?"

"We test drive this relationship until we decide if it's right for us."

"And if it isn't?"

"Then we part ways at least knowing we tried."

And risk a shattered heart. But what choice did she have now? He was right; she'd never be able to see him as just an assignment again. "Okay. But this is between us. No one else can know. We have to keep our relationship secret."

"That's—"

"Non-negotiable."

He looked at the ceiling for a moment then finally shrugged. "All right, if you insist. I talked with the pilot and we can't make the trip to Texas in one go. We have to stop for fuel several times and for them to rest. I have a little house in the Philippines. It's secluded, and no one will know where we are except the local population. Why don't we hole up there for a few days and enjoy ourselves without worrying about anyone seeing us. Max will love the beach."

Put off Texas for three days? Yes, please. Spend those three days with Daniel without worrying about being seen? Abso-bloomin-lutely.

"Sounds like a great plan."

Finally he smiled, and her heart ratcheted up another fifty beats per minute.

She would undoubtedly crash out completely before the end of the race. But until then she was going to enjoy every single thrill.

Chapter Twelve

Lexy strode down pit lane, clutching a computer tablet and trying to look official in her dove- gray suit. Except she still glowed from three days of complete heaven at Daniel's place in the Philippines. She'd expected a small shack. She got a lovely four-bedroom modern-style house with a private beach and staff to cook, clean, and basically find anything she needed.

Max had loved the beach. He'd been out there as soon as his breakfast was done and had had to be persuaded to come in for dinner. Genevieve had been a saint and kept him occupied with building sandcastles and playing pirate, so that Lexy could spend her time concentrating on Daniel. And vice versa. He'd pampered her, even painted her toenails, and made love to her in every possible location. If she'd had a sexual bucket list, she could now throw away the bucket. Although she had to admit, sex on the beach was a better drink than place to make love. She was sure she still had sand where sand should never be.

No matter what happened between now and the end of the season, she'd forever remember that time as the best in her life. However, as with all great things, it had to end, and they'd been in Texas for five days. To build Formula 1's fan base in the States, the drivers had all been required to do extra publicity and attend a variety of events—some formal, some easy-going like barbecues and fan rides in two-seater race cars.

Lexy had stayed as far in the background as possible. It was still a bone of contention between her and Daniel. He wanted her by his side; she wanted their affair to remain a secret. To be honest, it irked her no end to see so many women throw themselves at him. It wasn't his fault he was gorgeous and charming and sexy. Still, she wanted to grab the women vying for his attention by the hair and scream, "He's mine, so back off." Except she couldn't. And that irritated her more. All in all, she was a cactus in a bag being swung by an irate toddler. One wrong move and someone was going to get an arse full of prickles.

To top it all off there'd been another message from her boss, worrying over the lack of photos of Daniel with women. She'd emailed back that Daniel was working, so he couldn't party every day. But that hadn't appeased Mr. Petersen. He talked about flying out for the race. Would he call her bluff?

But all that had nothing on the fear that her ex-husband would show up out of the blue. Wesley's picture was in almost every paper as his father campaigned for the Republican nomination to run for president. Thankfully, Wesley had never shown any interest in Formula 1 during their brief marriage, and if she could leave Texas without him knowing she'd been there, she'd be able to breathe a hell of a lot easier.

Near the Ferrari garage she caught up with her father, who had just flown in that morning. Qualifying would start soon and she was going to watch it with him back at the hotel. She was way too emotional to stay on track, where everyone would see her feelings for Daniel. As well as she'd been able to conceal them so far, she knew when he was racing around the circuit it would be near impossible to hide how much she cared.

"Are you ready to go?" Papa asked after they exchanged kisses.

"Yes, I just wanted to wish Daniel good luck first," Lexy said as she looked around for her lover. Seemed he had the same idea because he was standing at the entrance to his garage, scanning the crowd as well. She waved to him and he rushed over.

She put a hand on his shoulder and then stood on tiptoe to whisper in his ear. The click of a digital camera alerted her to the paparazzi. Shit.

Daniel whipped his head around and glared at the photographer until he moved away. Damn, she didn't want Daniel to go into qualifying mad.

"I'll wait for our debriefing in our usual location," she said, using her best business voice in case anyone was listening.

"I trust it will be an in-depth, intense debriefing?" Daniel replied, his face creasing into his gorgeous smile.

Her breath caught in her throat and her voice came out way too sexy. "Of course. I'm very thorough."

She couldn't believe she was having this conversation in front of her father. Her face must be approaching Ferrari red about now.

"I look forward to our meeting. It's good to see

you again, Gian-Franco." The two men shook hands, although the real communication was in their eyes: her father warning him to tread carefully with his daughter, Daniel's saying he was doing the best he could. Another photographer snapped several photos of the three of them. Thank God Max was at the hotel with Genevieve.

In the end, Daniel only took second position on the grid, each of his laps compromised by some small error. She hurried to his room, anxious to get there before the rest of the F1 crews returned to the hotel and spotted her. How could she ease his frustration? She knew he worried that their relationship would affect his driving. And now it seemed it had. Would he even want to see her?

As she rounded the corner to his room, she was blinded by flashes of light. What the hell?

A throng of reporters rushed toward her, some snapping photos as they went, others holding their phones up to catch her every word.

"Alexandra, how long have you and Daniel Michaud been lovers?"

"Are you brokering a deal for Daniel to drive for Ferrari next year?"

"Are you the mother of Daniel's love-child? Who's the boy travelling with you?"

The questions came at her like missiles, each one hitting its mark.

"Are you in love with him?"

"Have you set a wedding date yet?"

"You were missing for three days between Russia

and Texas. Where were you?"

"What does Gian-Franco think of his daughter dating a driver from a rival team?"

"Are you leaking secrets between the teams?"

She clapped her hands over her ears in a vain attempt to stop the questions. The pack hounded her down the hallway until she made it back to her room. Thank God she'd insisted that she and Daniel have separate rooms, even though they spent every night together.

Heart pounding, she pulled out her phone to send a text to Daniel to warn him of the media maelstrom. A message popped up from her boss: Look on the internet. Pick me up at the airport at 11.30 a.m. tomorrow.

Her hands shook so much it took two goes to enter her name into the search engine.

"Daniel Michaud's Mystery Lover Revealed" followed by photos of her and Daniel in Russia, and the ones just taken on the grid that afternoon. But what stalled her heart was a photo of Daniel carrying Max out of the hotel in Sochi. "They even have a son!"

She had to get Max out of here now.

***

Daniel strode through the hotel lobby, still in his racing overalls. Lexy's text had sounded frantic, and it had been the first of many messages he'd received on the breaking "news." He had to reassure his team principal that he wasn't signing with Ferrari for next year.

Although it was probably every driver's dream to race the red cars at least once in their career. That dream would die a quick death if he screwed this up, whatever it was, with Lexy.

Was it a good thing their relationship was finally out in the open? He'd hated all the sneaking around and having to fake interest in other women when his whole body was consumed with her. He'd never known a physical relationship could bring with it so much emotional satisfaction. Or was it the other way around? But now the speculation on his performance would include questions as to whether he was distracted by his personal life. Questions that were already echoing through his head. He was off his game this weekend as it was. This was only going to make it worse.

He approached the concierge desk and requested that they send security up to clear his floor of reporters. They'd probably have to make some sort of statement to calm things down, but he wanted to know how Lexy felt it should be played. The hint that they had a child together was going to be the most devastating. She'd already been on edge enough in her ex-husband's home state. Chances were she'd be packed and gone before sunset.

As he headed toward the bank of elevators a tall, thin man put a hand on his shoulder. Daniel shrugged it off and turned to glare at the guy. He looked closely at the man again. They'd met briefly at a corporate reception earlier in the week. One that Lexy had refused to attend. As Daniel struggled to remember his name, he realized the man had the same color eyes as

Max. *Dieu*, this couldn't be Lexy's ex, could it?

"I am Wesley Harding the third," the guy said.

Three things flashed through Daniel's head instantaneously: Lexy had lied to him about who she'd been married to; he wanted to punch out the lights of the man who had treated Lexy so abysmally; and he needed to keep Lexy and Max safe. Beating this asshole probably wouldn't accomplish the last one, so Daniel put it on the shelf for the moment. Besides, blood was damn hard to get out of his overalls.

As much as it made his gut churn, he had to behave. "What can I do for you, Mr. Harding? I'm rather busy."

"I understand you know Alexandra Camparelli."

Given their photos splashed all over the internet, there was no point denying it. "We're colleagues working on a project."

"According to my newsfeed, you're more than that. As one rich man to another, I feel the need to warn you. She's a gold-digger. Took me for a cool million. I don't know what hooks that gal's got into you, but get out now while you're still solvent."

Lexy had not only lied about having been married to a nobody, but also about her divorce settlement. Daniel's chest burned like the worst case of acid reflux he'd ever had. It took effort to breathe. "I'll listen to Alexandra's side of the story, but thanks for the heads-up."

"She's a real smart girl, that one. If y'all don't believe me, ask my money people. They cut her the check." Wesley followed Daniel across the lobby. No way was he going to have this conversation with Lexy with her ex in tow.

Before he could excuse himself, an elevator door opened and Lexy rushed out, Max in her arms with a Ferrari ball cap pulled way down over his brow. It should have pleased Daniel that she wore his team's hat, but he was too caught up with the sheer panic on her face. Genevieve hurried behind, dragging a suitcase.

"Mr. Harding, why don't we get a drink and you can tell me what happened," Daniel said, trying to distract the man so Lexy could make her escape. Too late. Wesley caught sight of her and stepped into her path.

"Holy shit. Is that my boy?" Shock kept Wesley's voice low. Even so, several people stopped to watch the little drama playing out in the lobby.

Daniel stepped between Lexy and her ex. "If you don't want this entire conversation aired on the evening news, I suggest we take this discussion somewhere private." He put a hand on Wesley's arm to prevent him coming any closer to Lexy.

"I have nothing to say to him," Lexy replied. Daniel's stomach fell. Any hope that she didn't know this guy evaporated at her words. How could she not tell him she'd married into one of America's heavyweight political families? Wesley Harding III did not count as "no one important."

"Alexandra, is that my son?"

She shifted Max to her other hip, farther away from his father. Camera phones were out now, recording the scene.

"Lexy, Wesley, look around," Daniel said as quietly as he could. It broke them out of their stare-down, and for the first time they noticed the audience.

"Oh, God." Lexy paled and Daniel put an arm around her.

The concierge appeared at his side. "Mr. Harding, Mr. Michaud, our business center is currently empty if you'd like some privacy. It's just this way." He directed them to an office to the left of the lobby.

Lexy had such a tight hold on Max, the little boy struggled to breathe. Daniel took him out of her arms, but still he wheezed. "Lexy, where's Max's inhaler?" While she searched in her bag, Daniel turned to the concierge. "Get a bottle of water. And a whiskey," he added after glancing at Lexy's face. All her nightmares were coming to light in one afternoon. He wanted to take her in his arms and tell her everything was going to be okay. But at this point, he'd probably be lying.

Finally finding the asthma medicine, Lexy gave it to Max. Within a minute his breathing became easier. "Genevieve, take Max back upstairs. Call us immediately if he has another attack," Daniel instructed.

"Wait one dad-gum minute—" Wesley began as he moved to block the door.

"Touch the boy or his mother and that's the last thing you'll do," Daniel threatened.

Wesley moved aside, his gaze never leaving Max's face as Genevieve took him from Daniel. He opened the door at the same time the concierge returned with the drinks. "Please have security escort Ms. Dubois and the child back to her room," Daniel said then handed the bottle of water to Max, the whiskey to Lexy, and shut the door again. With her son safely out of the room, Lexy sank into a chair.

"Alexandra, why the hell didn't you tell me I had a child? Momma never would have insisted on a divorce if she knew you were carrying her grandchild. And you should have named him Wesley. You know that's the tradition in my family." Wesley leaned over the table but made no move to get closer to her.

"His name is Maximillian Camparelli. And he's my son. Not yours." Lexy slung back the whiskey, returning color to her cheeks.

Wesley's eyes narrowed. "Are you saying you had sexual relations with another man while you were married to me?"

"I'm saying you make one move to take my child from me and I'll cut off your prized family jewels, as pathetic as they are, and feed them to your daddy's cattle. Although I doubt they'd want them either." Lexy stood and Wesley took a step back. "I think we're done here."

"Don't count on it, darlin'. My lawyers will be in touch." With a sneer, Wesley strode from the room, his phone already at his ear.

Daniel shut the door again. "You told me you were married to no one important." He paced the room the other side of the table from Lexy. "The Hardings do not qualify as unimportant. How the hell did you wind up with him?"

"When we met, I honestly didn't know who he was. My mum only watched trashy dramas and reality TV, and we never followed American politics. And at uni I was so intent on my studies and weight-loss, I never paid much attention to what was happening in the world."

"You met at university?" He was still reeling from the knowledge that Lexy had been involved with one of the most powerful families in America. No wonder she'd been so paranoid. If she'd have trusted him, Daniel never would have asked her to come to Texas. She could have stayed in the Philippines and then met him in Mexico.

"Yes. Wesley came to Cambridge to finish his economics degree. We literally ran into each other while we were reading and walking. He was shy and quiet and so was I. I'd lost most of the weight by that time, but I still didn't have any self-confidence. I guess he liked the fact that I had no clue about his family. We started going out, and after four months he asked me to marry him."

"Did you love him?" The burn in his chest ignited again as he waited for her answer.

"I thought I did. I'd never had a man even look at me before. I was flattered, and convinced myself this was my only chance to get married. He never talked about his family, so I assumed he was estranged from them, like I was. We married in the registrar's office with only the staff there as witnesses."

"And how long did the marriage last?"

"Three months. And to be honest, it was bloody

awful. When we were going out he'd treated me like a princess. But that all changed once his ring was on my finger. He was so lazy, couldn't even pick up his clothes and put them in the laundry hamper. He never helped with cooking or washing up. I was his personal servant. And the sex was pathetic."

"Lexy, don't…" Daniel didn't want to hear about her with another man.

"Please. I've never told anyone, not even Sonia. I'd like to get it off my chest." Without waiting for his reply, she continued, "We were both virgins when we married. And he hated my body, said it was gross. After I went to bed, he'd watch porn then he'd come upstairs and wake me up for sex. He kept the lights off so he didn't have to look at me and left my nightie on so he didn't have to touch my skin. It was nothing like what we share. I'd never even had an orgasm till I met you."

He really wished he'd punched Wesley now. "*Mon Dieu*, tell me you tossed that asshole out the door."

"I wish. Somehow, his mother got wind of our marriage and showed up at the house on our three-month anniversary. She didn't say a word to me, just dragged Wesley out into the garden. Then ten minutes later, they both left."

"What? He didn't talk to you, explain what was happening?"

"Just, 'Sorry, darlin', this has been a mistake. You can stay here until the lease runs out next month.'"

How could a man treat a woman that way? Especially a woman he professed to love enough to marry?

"What did you do?"

"I moved back to student digs, and two weeks later I received a package by courier with a document dissolving the marriage and a check for a million dollars. I signed the paperwork but didn't cash the check. It made me feel like he was paying for my services in bed and out. Trust me, our marriage, and especially the sex, was not worth that much. Then the next day I discovered I was pregnant. Wesley never even bothered to contact me, so I never told him about the baby. If he didn't want me, he wasn't having my child. And I felt like if accepted his financial offering, he'd have bought a right to Max as well."

"Wesley claims you took his money. That's why he was here, to warn me you were a gold-digger."

"That lying bastard."

He caught her gaze and held it. "Why didn't you tell me the identity of Max's father? Don't you trust me?"

"I … I don't know. I guess I thought it would change the way you saw me. That maybe you would think I'm a gold-digger like Wesley claimed. You'd already accused me of trying to sleep with you to get pregnant and demand child support."

He stared at her. Did he see her differently? Why did it matter that the asshole she'd been married to was a billionaire with immense political connections and not just some douche who didn't know a real woman when he had one?

"I promised I would never jeopardize your custody of Max, but you neglected to tell me the one vital piece of information that would allow me to live up to that vow." He ran a hand through his hair, shocked to find it shaking. "I've explored every inch of your body, but you haven't really let me in, have you, Lexy?"

"Daniel … I…" Her hand that had reached out to him dropped back into her lap. She had no excuse.

"*Merde*. What do you want to do about the rest of this mess? There's no point denying our relationship now; they've pieced together the photos from Russia and figured out you're the woman in all of them."

She sighed. "I know. And my boss is on his way here. I guess the shit will fully hit the fan tomorrow."

He scrubbed his hands over his face, suddenly bone weary. "I have a race to win, and from second place on the grid. This is the worst timing possible."

"I'm sorry. I know this is a distraction you don't need."

He pulled in a deep breath, trying to release some of the tightness in his chest. "I'm going to have a quiet night in my room. I'll see you tomorrow. Do you want me to hire a bodyguard for you and Max?"

"No. I don't think Wesley will try anything. At least not without consulting Momma this time."

His hand was on the door handle when Lexy's shattered voice stopped him.

"Are we done?" The question sliced through him.

"I don't know. We'll talk tomorrow after the race."

Chapter Thirteen

Mr. Petersen looked straight at her then scanned the crowd again. As he passed within a foot she heard him mutter something under his breath about incompetent staff. No way was she going to continue working for him. Daniel was right; she did have options. What they were she wasn't sure, but she'd figure it out. Life was too short to do something she hated.

She stepped out of the crowd and grabbed her boss's arm. "Welcome to Texas," she said.

He looked her up and down and then once again for good measure. "I didn't recognize you. You've done something to your hair … and, well, you look nice." *Be still my beating heart. With compliments like that I could lose my head.*

It'd taken an hour to do her makeup this morning, hiding the ravages of a sleepless night. And if Genevieve hadn't cancelled her second room service order, Lexy would be dealing with a food binge hangover as well. She'd alternatively worked herself into a frenzy thinking that any second Wesley was going to show up at her door with the police, demanding she hand over Max, then relaxed, remembering that her ex didn't have the balls to claim his own socks at the Laundromat, never mind his son. Still, she had asked Genevieve to stay in the hotel room with Max and not open the door to anybody but her, Daniel, or her father.

Lexy'd had a brief conversation with her father last night as well. She'd come clean to him about Wesley, and he'd promised to stand beside her if it came to a custody fight. Ferrari was also going to issue a press statement saying it had not approached Daniel Michaud with a driving contract.

"Do you have a checked bag? The race starts in a couple of hours and we need to get to the track. I have a VIP pass for you so you'll be able to get something to eat and drink there." She was anxious to get to the circuit. Daniel had left for final practice early this morning after only a quick kiss. She could tell his mind was already on the circuit. At least he'd come by to check if she was okay. And he'd asked her to watch the race from his garage. That had to mean something, right?

"No, I just have my carry-on."

"Good." She directed him to a town car waiting by the curb.

"You're sleeping with him, aren't you?" Mr. Petersen barely waited for the driver to shut the door before asking.

"Yes."

"That is completely the opposite of what you were told to do. I can fire you."

Go ahead, make my day. "How I conduct my personal life is none of your business, Mr. Petersen. However, as far as Destin Designs in concerned, I have a proposal for you to present to them."

"What is that?" His tone shifted from accusatory to intrigued.

"In all the photos the media have of me and Daniel together, I'm also wearing Destin Designs creations. My understanding is that their women's wear line is not doing so well. So, while I'm not saying I'm the ideal model, we can spin it that it took a woman wearing Destin Designs to capture the attention of the international playboy."

God, she hated turning her relationship into an advertising campaign, but it should keep the client happy, Daniel would still be able to get his payout—money he'd promised to a girls' education campaign—and it would hopefully buy her some time to figure out what she was going to do next.

"That could work," Mr. Petersen acknowledged. "I'll call them tomorrow."

She itched to tell him to take his job and stick it where the sun didn't shine, but she wasn't that reckless. Not yet, anyway. She needed a plan first. She'd seen firsthand what happened when a woman relied solely on a man. If this didn't work out with Daniel, or God forbid, something happened to him, she had to have a career, or at least a job, to fall back on. She would not end up like her mother.

Thanks to their VIP passes, they cut through many of the lines and she managed to ditch Mr. Petersen in the hospitality room well before the parade lap. After introducing him to several of the people she knew, she sneaked out to Daniel's garage. He was already in his car on the grid and most of the mechanics were hovering there. As soon as the fifteen-second warning was given, they'd remove the tire blankets and race back to the pit lane. Adrenaline coursed through her, but she knew it was nothing compared to what they were feeling. How did they cope with so much stress in their job? Their performances were measured in thousandths of a second.

Twenty minutes into the race, Lexy wasn't sure she was going to make it. She smiled for the cameras as they came around, cheered when Daniel made a pass, held her breath during the pit stops, and basically functioned at a cellular level during the rest of the time. Caring for a man who put his life in danger to win a stupid trophy was ridiculous. As Mandy had predicted, she felt every curve, every dip in the track as though she were in the car as well. At least watching from the garage, where food wasn't allowed, meant she couldn't give in to her craving for a fully-loaded pizza and a bathtub-sized margarita.

When Daniel eventually finished in second place, she collapsed onto her chair, only to have to run the length of the pit lane in high heels in order to catch a glimpse of him before he ascended to the podium. How could she do this week after week? Year after year? She'd have a heart attack by the time she was thirty.

If she stayed with Daniel. They still had to talk.

***

Daniel forced a smile. Second place was just the first loser. As he sprayed the champagne on the crowd below, he spotted Lexy. His chest swelled and his heart rate sped up. He could blame his second place finish on her or all the distractions from yesterday, but it didn't change anything. He was damned if he did and damned if he didn't, so he might as well do her. Too bad it hadn't stayed at that. Whatever it was he felt for her, it was a hell of a lot more complicated than mere lust.

She waved up at him and his smile became genuine. With only one week before the race in Mexico, he'd better get this sorted *rapidement*.

"Did I cost you the win?" Lexy asked several hours later when they were finally alone. She stood across the room from him, her arms crossed over her stomach. Her hair was swept up in intricate folds, and the green gown she wore showed her gorgeous curves to full advantage. They were due at the victory party in twenty minutes.

"No. I've finished in second place before. I never got it together this weekend. There's no one to blame but myself." Some of the tension left his shoulders. It was true; he hadn't been in sync with his car or the track. Some weekends were just like that. Overanalyzing did nothing but give him a headache. It was better to put all his energies into winning the next race. "How are you doing?"

"Okay. I'll be happy to leave Texas. I haven't heard anything from Wesley or his lawyers. Mr. Petersen is schmoozing potential clients. He threatened to fire me for sleeping with you and for bringing Max with us. However, as our personal relationship is none of his business, and as he never specifically said I couldn't bring my son with me, he doesn't have a case for dismissal on either count. And, you are now looking at the new, albeit very temporary, face of Destin Designs's women's fashion division."

"You wear it well. Their profits are bound to skyrocket. But I asked about you. How are you coping?"

"I ate two hamburgers last night and would have had more if Genevieve hadn't intervened. But so far today all I've had is a banana and a salad. And eight fingernails," she added with a shrug.

He moved over to her and then ran his fingers down her cheek. "Were you worried about me?"

"Of course I was—" The rest of her reply was lost in his kiss.

"Let's not do that again, okay?" he said as he kissed down her neck and let his fingers trace the v-neckline of her dress until they came against the firm swell of her breasts.

"Not do what?" Her head was flung back, one hand was in his hair, and the other clutched his shoulder.

"Not sleep apart. It was hell." His lips traced the path his fingers had taken moments before.

"Agreed. But don't you think we'd better get to the party?"

He raised his head, satisfied that Lexy's eyes were now glazed with passion and not clouded with worry as they'd been when she entered the room. "The only good thing about not winning is that I don't have to stay so long at the after party."

"I don't recall you staying long after you won in

Russia," she reminded him.

"Touché. At least this time if we get photographed making out, it will be old news and no one will care."

She gave him a stern look, one she used on Max when he was about to do something naughty. "Maybe you should just keep your hands to yourself."

He laughed. "With you around? Not going to happen."

And it didn't. By the time they made it back to his room two hours later, they were both gasping for breath.

"Daniel." Lexy moaned his name as he cupped her breasts, his thumbs and forefingers rolling her already tight nipples.

"Hmm?"

"You are always a winner to me."

***

His luck completely broke in Mexico. After passing one of the slower cars, the driver missed his braking point for the corner and hit Daniel in the rear, spinning him into the Armco barrier. His car was damaged; he was out of the race.

"You okay?" the voice of his chief mechanic came through his ear piece.

"Yeah, I'm okay. I think the rear suspension is broken."

"Sorry, mate." Not as sorry as he was.

The track marshals surrounded his car and he had to leave his beloved Eva behind. He waved to the crowds as he made his way to the garage on the back of a moped. Despite being out of the race, he stayed at the track and helped the team get Robert, his teammate, home in first position. After finishing second in Texas, Daniel had been fourteen points ahead in the championship. But with today's non finish, Robert surged ahead and was now eleven points in front. Fortunes changed quickly in this sport. He had to win both remaining races to clinch the title. Second place wouldn't cut it anymore.

What if this drop in form continued? Even before the accident, he'd been fighting the car, not driving it. All he'd ever wanted to be in life was an F1 driver. Without his career, what was he? Just a pretty boy who liked to read. He pushed the issue to the back of his mind. It had to be the Did Not Finish making him question everything. But the malaise was twice as bad as it had been in Texas.

"Daniel, I must speak with you."

He turned to see Gian-Franco strolling toward him, his eyes narrowed and his mouth a firm, hard line. *Dieu*, Daniel was not in the mood for a "what are your intentions toward my daughter" talk. 'Cause hell if he knew at the moment.

Daniel forced a smile and unclenched his fists. "I'm surprised you're not at the podium ceremony, with one of your drivers placing."

"This is more important." Gian-Franco crossed his arms over his chest, his stance suggesting that the race wasn't the only thing Daniel was going to lose today. "You think that if you weren't involved with

Alexandra, you would have won the race." It was an accusation, not a question.

"I never said that. It was a racing incident. They happen all the time." *Just not usually to me.*

"I can read your body language. I've been involved with this sport since before you were born. I know how drivers think. They always look for a reason to explain a bad day so they can avoid it next time. Have you ever crashed out in a race before?"

"You know I have."

"Ever finished second or worse?"

"Of course."

Gian-Franco took a step closer. "Were you sleeping with my daughter at those times?"

"No, sir." Daniel held his ground, not quite sure where this conversation was heading.

"Then don't put your current lack of form down to her or your relationship. You are a professional driver. One of the best I've ever seen. Your talent is amazing. But even the most talented sportspeople have off days. Listen to a man who has made more wrong choices than right. A good woman doesn't make a man weak. She makes him stronger. Now, put today behind you and win the damn race in Rio."

That meant a lot coming from a man who represented a rival team. "Thank you."

Gian-Franco waved and then hurried towards the Ferrari garage.

By the time Daniel returned to the hotel, his body felt heavier than a Humvee. Gian-Franco's words were slowly sinking in. Today's incident had nothing to do with his relationship status, but he wasn't up to being sociable. He knew, though, that Max would want to tell him all about his afternoon at the track with Lexy. Daniel could still remember the first race he'd attended and how he'd told every single staff member at the chateau that he was going to be a driver one day.

He slid the key card into the lock and opened the door, bracing himself for Max's onslaught. The room was silent. Maybe Lexy had taken Max and Genevieve out, guessing that he'd want some quiet time. Except he didn't really want to be alone; he'd like to hold Lexy. Now that their relationship was out in the open, he wanted to spend every moment possible with her.

Striding into the sitting room, he stopped. Where the sofa had been now stood a massive tent made out of the cushions and several blankets. As he stared, Lexy's head appeared out of the top.

"I made a fort. Come inside," she said before disappearing.

He kicked off his shoes and jacket and crawled under a blanket. "Where's Max?" Surely she'd made the tent for him.

"I got him and Genevieve their own room for the night. I told Max you would be sad your car got broken and you'd need some quiet time."

"And you built me a sofa fort?"

"I built you an amazing sofa fort. Come on, this is the best fort you've seen in a long time, isn't it? And you were the one who told me that men are just boys with bigger toys. When Max is sad, a fort always cheers him up. I thought I'd give it a try."

It was kind of working. A small smile twitched at the side of his mouth. “What do we do in this amazing sofa fort? You obviously have more experience than I do.”

“Well, I’ve got a few refreshments.” She pulled a room service tray out from under the coffee table. She’d ordered chocolate chip cookies, potato chips, popcorn, and some mini pizzas, all things he normally denied himself during the race season. But beside the kids’ assortment of foods was a bottle of whiskey and two glasses. “And I picked up that book you wanted to read.” She slid him a copy of Harper Lee’s last novel.

“So we eat junk food and read?” He grabbed a handful of popcorn then put a few kernels into her mouth when she opened to answer.

“That’s what I do with Max. But the one thing about sofa forts is that they get kind of warm. So in this adult version, clothing is optional.”

She unbuttoned her blouse and slid it off her shoulders. He could see the outline of her nipples against the white lace of her bra. Next she shimmied out of her trousers, revealing the matching boy shorts.

He swallowed. “I really like your fort.” He traced a finger along the lace top of her bra. She drew in a shuddering breath, pushing her chest closer to him. He leaned over and sucked her nipples through the fabric. Threading her fingers through his hair, she held his head to her chest. Crashing had its compensations.

He slid off her underwear, and she unhooked her bra and tossed it with the rest of her clothes. She sat naked beside him, no longer ashamed of her body. He was going to make this last as long as the race should have. He poured a glass of whiskey, dipped his finger into it, and drew the outline of the track on Lexy's body. He then licked it off, spending a long time on the curves that encompassed her breasts.

"Daniel, please," she begged after the third lap. "Take your clothes off. I want to play, too." He slid a finger into her, massaging her from the inside.

"Not yet. You went to a lot of effort to build this fort. I'm going to reward you for it."

He took his time doing justice to her hot, wet heat. Her head was thrown back on the sofa base, her arms spread wide—all his to do with what he wanted. It didn't get much better than this. As he continued to lick and caress, her head thrashed from side to side, her hair in wild abandon around her. And when she orgasmed, she yelled his name. He may have lost the race, but he'd won the prize.

"My turn," she said when her body stopped vibrating.

"What?"

But she was already unbuttoning his shirt, her tongue flicking across his nipples as she unfastened his belt and slid down his zipper. He raised his hips to help remove his clothes. Before he could position her, her lips closed around him. "*Mon Dieu*, Lexy…"

It wasn't the first time she'd done this to him, but it still pulled him inside out. She was alternating between sucking and licking, her fingers caressing the inside of his thighs and higher when his phone went off. It took three rings before he recognized the distinctive tone he'd assigned to his brother, Jacques.

"I have to get that." He could barely get the words out of his throat—how could he talk to his brother?

He managed to locate his phone in his trouser pocket and pull it out. As he slid the icon to answer, Lexy resumed her torture. She kept her eyes on his as she slid her mouth up and down on him. If he wanted her to stop, he just had to say so.

He didn't.

"Hello?" he croaked out. This was going to be the shortest conversation ever.

"Daniel, I have great news. The crime boss Maya testified against is dead. We can come out of hiding now," Jacques said.

"That's fantastic." It was really great, but not as wonderful as what Lexy was doing to him now.

"Are you okay? You sound a bit odd."

"Fine. Just can't talk now. I'll call you tomorrow, okay?"

"Sure. We'll come to your race in Rio."

"Great. Bye."

He flicked the phone off, closed his eyes, and let the woman who meant as much to him as racing rock his world.

***

"Lexy?"

"Hmmm?" She didn't open her eyes. Didn't want to acknowledge that another day was starting. She just wanted to lay here next to Daniel and never move again. They were still in the sofa fort, blissfully naked and satiated after a night of lovemaking.

"I need your advice," Daniel said. He stroked a lazy hand up and down her back.

She opened one eye. "About what?" At his concerned expression she sat up and put a hand on his face, caressing his cheek.

"I'll start at the beginning."

"It's a very good place to start."

He smiled and she managed to pull in a deeper breath. "Earlier this year I received an email from a Santiago Alvarez, claiming he was my half brother and that our father wanted to meet me. Evidently, my alleged father has cancer and isn't expected to live long. His dying wish is to see me before he passes."

"How did you respond?"

"I ignored it at first. As a quasi-celebrity I get a lot of these requests to meet, even claims of being family. They all end in asking for money. I thought this was one of the same."

"But now you think it might be legit?"

"He's been emailing me regularly, so I finally looked him up. If he's the Santiago Alvarez I researched then he's rich in his own right. He doesn't need my money. Finally, two weeks ago he sent me details of a DNA test from himself and my father and asked me to also submit a sample. I did it while in Texas and, according to the results, it's not a scam."

"Oh my God, you've found your father. Haven't you ever wondered what he's like?"

"A bit, when I was a kid. But I was happy with

Jacques and his grandfather. I don't need more family."

"So, what advice do you want?"

"Until I met you, I had no interest in meeting him. But now, after your reunion with your dad and seeing how happy it's made you all, especially Gian-Franco… Should I go? Santiago wants me to fly to their estate in Mendoza, Argentina, after the race in Rio. Just for two days to meet my father."

"What are you worried about?"

"He's dying. Do I want to meet him only to lose him right away? What's to be gained by that?"

"For you, probably nothing, but can you imagine his relief? He'll be able to go to his grave at peace. You are an incredible man; your father will be so proud of you. I can understand him wanting to see you just once."

He paused. "Okay, I'll go as long as you'll come with me."

"I'm not sure I'm included in the invite. Plus, I can't leave Max and Genevieve."

"It's a package deal; I go with my entourage, or I don't go. Dude has come this far, I think he'd be crushed not to get to go to Argentina. Speaking of fathers, have you heard anything from weaselly Wesley?"

She swallowed. "Not yet. I'm hoping his advisors have told him that a nasty custody fight will ruin his father's chance of making it to the White House. No way will Wesley cross his parents."

"I think you're right."

"What about your other brother, Jacques? Weren't

you speaking with him last night?"

"He and Maya are coming to the race in Rio as well. I'll let them decide if they want to come to Argentina or not. Damn, I hope Jacques doesn't want his plane back. For a guy who started this journey alone, I seem to have accumulated quite a posse."

"How do you feel about that?"

His hand cupped her breast and he lowered his head. "Right now? Amazing," he said against her skin.

Don't fall for a good-looking man, because you'll never hold onto him.

Chapter Fourteen

Lexy paced. They'd arrived in Rio early that morning and gone on a quick sightseeing tour, but neither Max nor Genevieve had felt great so they'd returned to the hotel. Daniel had gone off to a meeting with his team. He was on edge as well. Eleven points behind in the championship meant he had to win both of the next races. Papa wasn't coming to the Brazil race, as he had commitments back in Italy. She was rather relieved because the last time she'd been in Rio with her father, it had been memorable for all the wrong reasons.

But what had her pacing the hotel room was the imminent arrival of Daniel's brother Jacques and his wife, Maya. It was stupid to be nervous, but somehow meeting people Daniel loved and respected was much more daunting than integrating with his entire F1 team.

Would they judge Lexy because she was a single mum, dragging her child around the world after a man she had no hope of holding onto? Because as great a time as she was having with Daniel, she was very aware that he hadn't mentioned the "L" word at all. The old song advising her that "it was in his kiss" was complete pants. Unless he said it out loud, she wouldn't believe it, via exchange of saliva or not.

So, what was holding her back from admitting her feelings? She'd known she was in trouble when he'd walked out her flat door weeks ago carrying Dude like he was the coronation crown. When Jacqueline had accused her of being in love with Daniel she hadn't denied it. But was she? She certainly went through the wringer while he was on track. And when he walked into the room it was like all the air was sucked out of her lungs. Her body came instantly alive, and for the first time in her life she was excited to start each day. Especially when it began with Daniel snuggled up next to her.

They had seventeen days left in their stipulated road trip. Thankfully, Destin Designs had been excited to capitalize on the increased sales her affair with Daniel had afforded them, and had latched on to the suggested campaign. They'd even sent her several new outfits to wear when in public with Daniel. Their relationship had been devalued to an advertisement.

Daniel had hinted he still wanted her with him after Abu Dhabi. But what about her job? Her studies? And could she really drag Max around the world because she had the hots for an F1 driver?

Said man walked into the room, and the questions dulled to an uncomfortable niggle. It was hard to think of negatives when he was near.

"Jacques just texted me. They've landed and will be here within thirty minutes or so, depending on traffic," Daniel said as he pulled her into his arms for a kiss.

When he eventually released her lips, she asked the questions that had been bugging her since she heard his brother and sister-in-law were coming, "What if we don't get on? What if they don't like me or think I'm not good enough for you?"

He laughed and kissed her again. "Not a problem. We tell them to get lost. I don't need Jacques. I've got a spare brother now."

He dipped his head to kiss her again when the bedroom door flung open and Genevieve raced out. "Lexy, Max can't breathe. I've given him his asthma inhaler three times and it isn't helping."

She ran into the room, Daniel right on her heels. Max sat on his bed, incredibly pale. "It's going to be okay, honey. We're going to get you some help to breathe, okay?" She sat on the bed and pulled him onto her lap, stroking his hair.

What kind of mother was she? Kissing a man while her son in the next room was dying.

"I'll call for an ambulance," Daniel said, picking up the hotel phone on the bedside table.

Max's lips had a bluish tint to them. She had to do something. Sitting here waiting was agonizing. "Let's go down to the lobby so the ambulance attendants can get to him quicker."

She bundled Max in a blanket, grabbed his favorite stuffie, and started toward the door. Except she had so many tears in her eyes, she stumbled over the bag she'd left in the hallway earlier.

"Here, let me," Daniel said. Reluctantly she handed her son to her lover. He rubbed a hand up and down Max's back as he walked, soothing him. Lexy pressed her fist to her mouth, trying to hold back the sobs. Max needed her to stay calm. If he saw how upset she was, it would make it worse for him.

"I'm coming, too," Genevieve said. "I can't wait here…" Her face was deathly pale, and Lexy didn't have the heart or the time to argue with her. It would be cruel to tell her she had to stay.

When they arrived in the lobby, a well-dressed man strode over to them. He looked so much like Daniel that Lexy did a double take. Which brother was this?

"Good evening, I'm Santiago Alvarez…" He took one look at Max and then at her face and asked, "How can I help?"

"We're waiting for an ambulance," Daniel said. "My son needs to get to the hospital." His face was fierce, his jaw set, his eyes daring anyone to get in his way, as though it really were his child in distress in his arms. If she weren't so worried about Max, she'd have kissed Daniel right there.

"Your son … I wasn't aware." Santiago stared at Max again then gestured toward the door. "There has been a big accident on the highway; many of the ambulances will be tied up there. It will be quicker if I take you to the hospital in my car. Come this way."

He was obviously a man used to being in charge. But Daniel didn't move. "Thanks all the same, but we don't know you."

"We are family. Do you think I would allow something to happen to my father's grandson?"

Daniel glanced at her and she said, "I don't care how we get there. Let's just go."

They followed a swiftly-moving Santiago through

the door. He was barking orders into his phone in Portuguese. "Here's my car," he said and flung open the back doors to a limo.

As Lexy was about to step in, the car behind began to honk its horn furiously. Daniel glanced back and then handed Max to her. "One second," he said, and then true to his word he was back before she could even get her seatbelt on. Santiago knocked on the driver's partition.

"That was Jacques and Maya in the car behind. They're going to follow us. Looks like we'll have our family reunion in the hospital," Daniel said.

"I—" Lexy began.

"Don't even think of apologizing. This is what family does. And you're family now." He put his arm around her and with his other hand stroked Max's hair. He still struggled to draw a breath, but his lips hadn't turned any bluer and he was alert.

At the hospital, Santiago jumped out of the car first, calling out orders as he went. Two orderlies rushed out with a gurney and took Max from her. He cried and held out his arms, afraid she would leave him. She held on to his chubby hand and ran alongside. They were whisked into a private room immediately.

"Step aside, Lexy. Let them work," Daniel said as he gently pulled her away so the doctor could do his examination.

"I'm right here, Max, honey. I'm not going anywhere," she said as she let his hand go. She pulled in a shuddering breath and Daniel wrapped his arms around her. Santiago translated the doctor's questions and Lexy had to push past the lump in her throat to make her voice work. This wasn't the first time Max had been rushed to the hospital with an asthma attack. At least before, she'd been in her home country. What if they were somewhere where neither she nor Daniel spoke the language and he didn't have a handy half brother to assist?

They gave Max a nebulizer and within seconds his lips returned to a healthy pink. As the nurse hooked him up to the monitoring machines, Santiago explained to Max in a soft, gentle voice what they were doing and saying.

Max's blue eyes were huge as he watched all the adults in the room, but he didn't cry or complain when the nurse drew a vial of blood. Lexy was so proud of his courage, and struggled to keep her own tears inside.

"He's going to be fine," Santiago translated for the doctor. "They want to keep him here for a few hours to make sure. They'll give him some medicine but suggest that maybe Rio is not the best place for him. Their air quality is not good at the moment. It would be better for him to stay somewhere else."

"Maybe we can go with Jacques to where he's been living," Daniel suggested. He ran his hand up and down her arm and she leaned into his strength.

"I have a place in the countryside, near the mountains," Santiago said. "The air is pure and you will be most welcome to stay until your son recovers. I came to invite you to come there after the race to meet our father. I have a private plane and can have it ready to go as soon as they discharge Max."

Daniel looked his brother up and down. Lexy had to admit, as far as first meetings went, this had been a doozy.

At the moment, she just wanted Max safe. "I don't mind where. Daniel, I trust you to decide." She was turning over control of her son's welfare to him. It was a big step for her. And another sign she was losing part of herself to this man.

***

Daniel sucked in a deep breath. Max was going to be okay. That was the main thing. He'd been terrified when he'd seen the little boy's blue lips and the panic in Lexy's eyes. How had she coped all those months after Max's birth when they weren't sure if he was going to live or not? He'd gone through forty-five minutes of anxiety and he was a wreck.

Could he do this on a permanent basis? Because there was no Lexy without Max. And he wouldn't want there to be. But was he ready to be a father? Calling Max his son had just slipped out in the heat of the moment. Obviously the idea had been growing in his heart for a while now. Was it too late to let go? Could he?

"Lexy, I'm going to discuss this with my … brothers. I'll be back in a minute." *Dieu*, this was weird suddenly having family he never expected. But Santiago had been extremely helpful. It would have been more stressful without him there.

Santiago followed him out of the treatment room

and they found Jacques and Maya with Genevieve in the waiting area. As soon as he was two meters away, Maya launched herself at him, hugging him like he'd disappear if she didn't hold on.

"I'm so happy to see you, I'm not even going to question why you have two women and a child with you," Maya said.

Jacques was next in line to embrace him. "I'm happy to see you, too. Shame you've gotten even uglier. But I will ask, what the hell? I leave you alone for one year and you go all sister wives?"

"That's a long speech for an old married man. Sure you don't want to sit down now?" Daniel replied.

"Seriously, Daniel," Jacques said, his arm still around his shoulders. "Some introductions would be helpful."

Daniel hauled in a deep breath. "You know Genevieve. The little boy having the asthma attack is Max and his mother is Lexy, with whom I'm … involved." Lame term but "having a torrid love affair that I want to spin into a more permanent relationship but she insists is only a temporary fling" seemed too involved for the current discussion. "Genevieve has been Max's nanny while Lexy has been working. It's a long story and one I'll tell you over a bottle of wine, or two. And this," Daniel gestured Santiago forward, "apparently is my brother by another mother. We share a father, according to a DNA test."

"Who needs DNA? One look and anyone can see you're brothers," Maya said. She stepped forward and kissed a startled-looking Santiago on the cheek as well.

"I'm Maya. Welcome to the family. Or are we invading yours?" She shrugged and looked like she was going to kiss him again when Jacques grabbed her hand and pulled her back into his arms.

Jacques held out his hand and Santiago shook it. They both took the measure of the other and seemed satisfied with what they saw, although Jacques's arm tightened possessively around his wife. Daniel took a good look at his new brother for the first time. Santiago was tall, halfway between himself and ginormous Jacques. They had the same dark brown hair, but Santiago's eyes were more on the hazel side than green. But their nose and jawline were duplicates. It would be hard to deny they were brothers.

"Thank you. I look forward to getting to know you all." Santiago's eyes lingered a moment longer on Genevieve than anyone else.

"The doctors say Max is going to be fine but that he shouldn't stay in Rio because of the pollution. Jacques, is your place nearby? Can he and Lexy go there?"

"It's in Chile. Not too far, but it took us four hours by air. Then again, I had to hire a plane because you've got mine."

"Hey, you disappeared and left the keys."

"Jacques, I know you're excited to see your brother, but let's concentrate on the little boy. How would you feel if it were your child?" Maya rubbed her belly. Was she? From the rapturous look on his brother's face and the softening in Maya's eyes, Daniel was going to be an uncle soon.

“My country place is closer and I, too, have a private plane that could accommodate everyone,” Santiago offered.

“I don’t want to start off on the wrong foot,” Daniel said. “But we’ve just met. I’m not comfortable trusting two of the most important people in my life to you until I know you better. Unfortunately, I can’t leave Rio.” After the last two races, he would crawl around the track on his knees if he needed to in order to win.

“May I make a suggestion?” Maya asked but then carried on as if everyone agreed. “You trust Jacques with your girlfriend and her son, don’t you, Daniel?” He nodded. “If it’s okay with Santiago, why don’t all of us go to his place and wait for Daniel to join us after his race? That’ll give Max time to recover, and Jacques can make sure your harem is safe.”

It was the most logical solution. But Daniel still wasn’t happy about sending Lexy away with his new half brother. The guy was rich and apparently handsome, judging by the star-struck look on Genevieve’s face. What if she fell for him and his less complicated life?

“That’s an excellent idea, Maya. My house has twelve bedrooms—there’s plenty of space for everyone. And I have a doctor and nurse in residence tending to my father … our father,” Santiago rectified, “so if Max has another episode, there will be medical staff on hand.”

Couldn’t argue with that. Although he’d like to. “I’ll go talk to Lexy and see if she agrees,” Daniel said.

Lexy was sitting on the bed, stroking Max's hair, when he found her. She agreed that going to Santiago's, as it was closer and where Daniel had planned to go after the race anyway, was the best option.

Now he just had to get his heart on board. Because sending Max and Lexy away was going to hurt.

***

Lexy stepped out onto the terrace, holding her bathrobe closed at the neck. The mountain air was much cooler than in Rio. The sun was just coming up over the horizon, but she hadn't been able to sleep. She could claim it was the unfamiliar bed and worry over Max, but he'd made a fast recovery and you couldn't even tell that he'd had an episode a day later. Her heart knew the lack of sleep was due to Daniel not being there.

She'd watched the qualifying with his family yesterday and noticed Jacques's eyes on her more than once as she'd held her breath. In the end, Daniel had only managed second position on the grid. He'd been upbeat about his chances in the race when she spoke to him on the phone last night, but she still longed to be there. If someone had asked her two months ago if she'd ever leave her son to be with a man, she'd have slapped them across the face.

"You love him, don't you?"

Lexy swiveled to find Maya leaning against the doorframe. Her red hair fell in disarray around her shoulders, her short satin wrap revealed her gorgeous long legs. The woman embodied sexy. But she was also friendly and natural, and so obviously in love with her husband it made Lexy smile just to watch them.

"Yeah. Didn't want to but it happened. This has really screwed up my life."

"Preaching to the choir, sister. Love is damned inconvenient. But also the greatest thing ever. So, what are you going to do about it?"

"I have no idea." Lexy ran a hand through her hair, which probably just made it stand on end. "I don't know if I can do this—following Daniel around the world. Living from one heartbeat to the next as he risks his life for his sport. And what kind of life will it be for Max? His health isn't great, and changing environments can lead to more attacks like he had in Rio."

"I can't give you the answers, Lexy. You have to decide for yourself. But if you choose to stay with Daniel then know you won't be alone. You've seen how this family pulls together. Jacques and I would be more than happy to look after Max if you went to races with Daniel in countries where you weren't comfortable taking your son."

"I don't know…"

"Go to Daniel. You're not going to figure it out sitting here."

"I can't. Max—"

"Has so many people here to love and care for him it's ridiculous."

"But how am I going to get there? The race is in seven hours."

"I'm sure Santiago would lend you his plane and pilot. He seems a nice guy. If not, Jacques will arrange something."

"It's too much to ask. And Daniel's coming here tomorrow anyway. Why couldn't he be an accountant who lives down the street from me?"

"Because then he wouldn't be the exciting, vibrant man who charmed your heart. Close your eyes." Lexy complied. "Where do you want to be this second?"

"In Daniel's arms."

"Right answer."

Lexy opened her eyes in time to see Maya stride back into the house. Even in bare feet she towered over Lexy. The woman was a force to be reckoned with. Jacques probably had never stood a chance of resisting her.

Five minutes later a sleepy-looking Jacques appeared at the door. With his hair messed and his jaw covered in stubble, he didn't look half as intimidating as in the daytime. But then his blue eyes narrowed on her. "I hear you want to be with Daniel when he races."

She nodded.

"Get dressed then. We'll be wheels up in half an hour."

He strode back into the house and Lexy raced to get ready. She was throwing a few things into her bag when there was a knock at her bedroom door. Without waiting for an invitation, Maya entered holding a gorgeous pair of shoes and a small gift bag. "I noticed we have the same shoe size so I'm lending these to you for Daniel's private victory celebration tonight. Tell him I said, 'Happy birthday.'"

"It's not his birthday."

"I know, but we were in hiding for his last one and didn't send a present."

"Okay, but I'm not sure the shoes will fit him," Lexy said. She peeked into the bag and heat infused her face. It was going to take a drink or two before she could wear that without going red everywhere.

Maya laughed and left the room. Twenty minutes later, Lexy was strapped into the leather seat of Santiago's private plane and heading back to Rio. To surprise her man.

I am not my mother.

Chapter Fifteen

Daniel sat in his trailer with his eyes closed, waiting for the knock to call him to the garage. He tried to focus on the track, to see every curve, anticipate every braking point and shift change in his mind. Except all he could see were Lexy's eyes smiling at him. *Merde*, this shouldn't be hard. He'd managed every race alone for almost two seasons with the exception of the last three, so why did he feel so bereft now? He'd always figured it would be having a woman in his life, not her absence, which caused a distraction.

The knock on his trailer door came and he got up, glancing briefly at the clock. Ten minutes early. Had the mechanics discovered something wrong with the car? It'd been fine this morning in final practice.

Expecting the burly, bearded face of his chief mechanic or even the practiced smile of the press relations woman, he was shocked to find Lexy standing outside the door. Had he begun to projecting her face on other people? *You're losing it, man.*

"Daniel." No, it was her voice, her sexy way of looking at him that sent his blood rushing around his body at twice the speed.

"Lexy. What are you doing here? Where's Max?"

"Still in Argentina with your family. He's fine. But I couldn't let you race alone."

A tsunami of emotion rolled over him, weakening his knees. Now was not the time to realize how much he needed this woman.

"Come in." *Dieu*, she was still standing on the pavement, three feet below him.

"I wasn't sure—"

He didn't wait for her to complete her sentence. Lexy and her doubts. He'd hoped she'd be over them by now. "I will always want to see you. Anytime, anyplace." He swept her into a kiss that lasted until the knock came, calling him to his car.

"Do you want to watch from here or with the team?" he asked as she straightened her clothes, which had become somewhat dislodged during their embrace.

"Garage. I promised Max I'd wave to him if I was on TV."

He escorted her down pit lane. How would he be able to concentrate, knowing that Lexy had voluntarily left her son to be with him? She must love him. Was now the time to tell her how he felt? The questions whirled in his mind until he pulled on his helmet. Then a peace descended and the track came into sharp focus. He was going to win; he felt it in his fingertips.

It was a hard-fought battle; several times he'd been wheel-to-wheel with Robert. After the last two races, he'd worried he'd be hesitant, second-guessing his instinct, but the racing adrenaline took over and he made lightning-quick decisions that paid off in the end. Best of all, he knew Lexy was waiting to congratulate him when it was all done.

She wasn't hard to spot from the podium in her

bright orange jumpsuit. What was harder was hiding his hard-on in his racing overalls when her breasts bounced as she jumped for joy with the rest of the crowd. No need to practice his media smile today, it was genuine happiness coursing through his veins. He congratulated Robert, who had taken second place. There were now only four points between them, so the winner of the next race would take the championship. With Lexy staring up at him, her face glowing, he felt like he'd already achieved it.

***

Lexy bustled through the lobby of the Grand Hyatt, forcing down the panic at the reminder of the last time she'd raced through there, Max barely breathing. He was fine. Genevieve had sent her a video of him dancing around the room when he saw on the telly that Daniel took the checkered flag.

While Daniel was busy finishing up interviews, Lexy wanted to get ready for their private victory celebration before the party tonight. She wasn't quite brave enough yet to don the PVC outfit Maya had sent—that might take a couple of drinks. But maybe a little sexy librarian role-play would do to start. She was just figuring out what to wear, or not wear, when a man's hand grabbed her arm.

A scream stuck in her throat as she looked into the blue eyes of her ex-husband. What was it with the man and hotel lobbies?

"Alexandra, I'm glad to catch you alone."

"I'm not. I thought I made myself clear; I never want to see you again, Wesley."

He let go of her but didn't move away. "I've done some thinking, and the best solution is for us to get remarried."

"What? Are you out of your mind? Our marriage was a disaster the first time. No way in hell would I put myself through that again."

"Not even for our son?" She hesitated for half a second and he pounced on that. "Hear me out. I've got a court order for a paternity test, and we both know what it's going to reveal. I'm Maximillian's father. I've gone over the photos of him, and there's a strong resemblance to me as a child. And think of the benefits for him and for you if we remarry. I've got money and a large house. You'll never have to work again, and Maximillian will have every advantage in life, get into any university, do anything he dreams. I have staff so you don't even have to clean. And you can do anything you want, even go back to school if that will make you happy. You wanted to be a research scientist in the neurological causes of food addictions, if I remember correctly. My family would fund your own research team. Imagine what you could do to help people like your mother. There would be no custody battle, no messy and expensive court proceedings. It would all be neat and tidy."

"But I don't love you," she protested.

"You did once; you can again if you try. I've grown up in the past four years, darlin'. I made mistakes the first time we were together, but I know I can make you happy. And you'll have our son and any other children you want to have."

A shudder sliced through her at the thought of Wesley touching her again, and her stomach roiled. She needed to buy time, make him think she was considering his offer while she worked out what to do, where to go. "Can I think about it? I'm contractually obliged to Destin Designs for the next three weeks. Can I give you an answer on December first?"

He searched her face then finally nodded. "Just make the right decision, Alexandra. I don't want to fight you for custody of my son, but I will if I have to." Wesley put his Stetson back on and sauntered out of the hotel.

Another tremor wracked her body. Say goodbye to the man she loved or give up her son? No matter what she decided, she lost. It would hurt to let go of Daniel but kill her to lose Max.

***

Daniel glanced over at Lexy as the plane landed at the small, private airstrip in Mendoza. She'd been distracted since he arrived at the hotel last evening. Sure, she'd tried to put on a brave face and pretend nothing was wrong. But there was. He knew it. She was shutting him out again.

She'd eaten her dinner and his, then followed it with a huge ice cream sundae. And she'd drunk way more than usual. At first he thought that perhaps she was just enjoying the freedom of not having Max near, letting loose and being herself. But as her behavior got more desperate and her attempt to out-party even the most diehard hedonist became apparent, he'd picked her up and carried her back to his hotel room. There he'd held her through the night as she battled her personal demons in her sleep.

"I wish you'd tell me what's wrong," he said as they made their way from the airport to his brother's house.

The smile she gave him was so tight it was virginal. "Nothing's wrong. I'm just tired."

Her lie slapped him across the face. Was it because he hadn't told her he loved her? Their initial relationship term was coming to an end, but surely she knew he wanted them to continue being together. Did she need some kind of commitment from him? Was he ready?

As the car drew up in front of a large Spanish-style mansion, half a dozen people stood out front and cheered. When he'd won his first championship, only Jacques and Grand-Papa had welcomed him. How many would be there to celebrate with him when he won the next? Because damn it, he was going to win.

Santiago stepped forward. "Welcome, Daniel. Our father wanted to be here as well, but he's having a treatment in his rooms. He'd like to see you as soon as you're ready."

Daniel nodded. Was he ready to meet his father? First he'd greet those he did know. He hugged Grand-Papa, who was much frailer than the last time he'd seen him. When he eventually let go, Jacques put his arm around his grandfather.

"Move out of the way, Daniel. I'm happy to see you, but it's your woman I really want to meet," Grand-Papa said, his blue eyes twinkling. At least some things hadn't changed.

Daniel turned to find Lexy climbing the stairs to enter the house. "She's not feeling great. Later, okay, Grand-Papa? I promise you'll love her as much as I do."

The question that really rattled him was if she loved him at all. Was she already pulling away?

"I'll go see if she needs anything," Maya said, and followed Lexy into the house.

Genevieve mentioned a special snack and both Max and Santiago's niece, Miranda, went with her. Grand-Papa joined them and Max grabbed his hand and chatted to him as they walked.

Which left him, Jacques, and Santiago standing in the drive. Brothers, but not.

Time to get it over with. "I'll see my father now," Daniel said. The word "father" felt strange on his tongue.

Santiago led the way into the house, down a long corridor, and then stopped in front of a set of double doors. "The doctor says it may be a matter of days before he passes. Thank you for coming. This means a lot to him."

His half brother knocked on the door then opened it without waiting for a reply. Inside, a hospital bed was surrounded by every hi-tech piece of equipment Daniel had ever seen. On all flat surfaces, at least two or three books were stacked. Finally, he forced his eyes to connect with the man lying in the bed. Daniel's knees wobbled before he locked them, unable to take another step into the room. It was like looking through a time warp, where he saw himself fifty years from now, the resemblance between him and his father startling.

"Papa." Santiago's voice broke a bit. He clearly loved his father. What would it have been like if Daniel had met him years earlier? Would they have shared a similar bond? "Daniel's here."

His father opened his eyes, the same shade of green as his. Daniel swallowed. Everything he'd planned to say, all the clever quips he'd thought of, fled. He blinked a couple of times and then forced his legs to propel him to the bedside.

"Hello, Mr. Alvarez." *Dieu.* Who greeted their father for the first time by using his last name?

"Please, call me Luis. Tiago, you don't need to stay." His father's voice was raspy but otherwise strong.

Santiago nodded. "Jacques wants to see the winery. Do you want us to wait for you, Daniel?"

"No, I prefer the product to the process. You go ahead; I'll catch up with you later."

Santiago kissed his father on the cheek before leaving the room.

"Please, come sit down." Luis pointed at a chair next to the bed. "I have been following your racing career since I realized you could be my son. But I would like to know a little about you personally."

"How did you come to think we were related?" It

was the question that had been bugging him since Santiago's first email.

"You look just like me when I was younger. I pray you don't look like me now when you're my age. Don't worry; the cancer is not hereditary. I smoked until a few years ago. When you won your first world championship, there was a big article on you in one of the magazines, your photo on the cover. Someone pointed out the likeness to me, and so I looked you up. It took a bit of digging, but eventually I found a photo of your mother and recognized her as the woman I'd had a weekend affair with around the time of your conception. There was never any mention made in your bio about a father."

"My mother never told me who my father was. She was married at the time you met her, but due to her husband's inability to procreate, she knew I wasn't his."

"I'm sorry. I didn't know she was married or I would never have… Anyway, I was in Paris for business, my wife had died, and I was lonely. Your mother approached me and one thing led to another. I tried to contact her, but she said I'd been only a fling; she wasn't looking for a relationship."

"Sounds like my mother."

"I'm sorry, Daniel. If I had known you had resulted from our affair, I would have asked for custody or at least access." A tear trickled down his father's face. Due to his mother's indifference, he'd missed out on a lifetime of paternal love.

"I had a good childhood. My half brother's

grandfather did an excellent job of raising me. Have you met him?"

"Yes, briefly. He's a good man. I am so glad you were loved." Luis's eyelids closed and he opened them again with effort. "I need to rest now. Perhaps you could call the nurse to read to me?"

"May I read to you? If you have an English or French book, that is. My Spanish is not worth listening to." And something he'd probably need to work on if he was to keep in touch with his new brother.

"You like to read?"

"After Lexy and racing, it's my next greatest passion."

Luis smiled. "Now I know you are my son."

Daniel searched through the books and found a copy of *The Great Gatsby* in English. He read until his father's head lolled to one side and the nurse came in to check his vitals.

"*Él duerme*," she whispered. *He's sleeping*.

Daniel slipped quietly out of the room and went in search of Lexy.

Chapter Sixteen

Lexy couldn't settle. Her whole body seemed to itch on the inside. The hangover was mostly gone, thank God, but it had left in its wake a terrible sensation that it was the beginning of the end. As much as she tried to dismiss Wesley's threats, what if he was right? What if it was the best for everyone? As much as she loved Daniel, how could it work out for them long-term? When Max started school, would she stay behind in England or France while Daniel continued racing? She was not going to end up like her parents. It would be better to end things now, while she still had fabulous memories and not the bitterness of clinging to a relationship that had died long ago.

"Excuse me; I'm going for a walk," she said to Daniel's father, Grand-Papa, and Maya. The four of them had been sitting on the terrace in the late afternoon sunshine. Maya had been entertaining the two older men with stories of her great-grandmother.

Daniel and Max were kicking a football around on the grass. Her son's squeals of delight for once didn't lighten her mood. Genevieve and Miranda were having a tea party complete with hats, feather boas, and gloves. Lexy had tried to join them earlier but as soon as she'd approached, Miranda's eyes had sunk to the ground and she'd stopped talking. It seemed Genevieve was the only one who could reach the little girl still traumatized after the death of her parents.

"Would you like to join us?" Santiago asked as she passed. He and Jacques were doing a blind taste test of a half dozen bottles of wine. The labels were covered and they were attempting to identify the grape varietals by taste alone. One sniff of wine and Lexy's stomach protested.

"Thank you, but no. I'll leave it to you experts. Okay if I wander around your gardens?"

"Please, be at home," Santiago replied.

She strolled around to the side of the house. Not because the flowers looked more interesting there, but because it would stop her staring at Daniel. More snippets of last night had come back to haunt her. Getting drunk was one thing—while it was a first for her, she was fairly certain it was a more common occurrence for others. It was the utter loss of control that worried her.

She was stroking the velvety petals of a rose when she sensed she was being watched. Daniel stood a few paces away, his hands thrust in the front pockets of his jeans. The look on his face said he wasn't sure if she wanted him near or not. She gave him a hesitant smile, and he closed the distance between them. None of this feeling of unease was his fault. He'd done everything possible to make her feel special and loved.

Daniel wrapped his arms around her and she snuggled against him. God, he felt so good. "Feeling better?"

"Much. I'm sorry about last night."

"Don't be. I've had a few nights like that as well."

"Are there pictures all over the internet?"

"Not any more. Jacques had his hacker guy delete them. He'll keep an eye out for the next couple of weeks, but these things blow over pretty quickly. There'll be someone else dancing naked in the fountain tomorrow."

"I didn't, did I?"

He paused and she glanced up at his face. "No, of course you didn't. I'm not about to let anyone else see what's for my eyes only." He kissed her leisurely before pulling back. He searched her eyes, worry clearly evident in his. A shiver coursed through her.

"Lexy, we have a problem." He said it with such seriousness she pulled back. Had Wesley talked to Daniel as well? Threatened to end his career if he didn't let her go? As gifted a driver as he was, he still relied on sponsorship. If the Hardings used their political clout to end that…

"What?" She held her breath.

"Dude is dead. I went to feed him this morning and he was belly-up in his bowl. Max is going to be devastated."

A slightly hysterical laugh erupted from her throat. All this worry for a fish? If only he knew what was really at stake. "We are currently on Dude version 6.0. I'll just tell Max he's resting and get another one as soon as we get to a town."

"Oh, good."

"Were you really upset about a fish?"

"As much as I hate to admit it, Dude and I have

had some pretty intimate moments over the past few weeks."

"True. I was a bit jealous of that fish."

He put both hands on his cheeks, his eyes huge. "*Mon Dieu*, you didn't kill him, did you?"

She laughed again, more genuinely this time, and snuggled into his chest. Damn, she was going to miss this—his strong arms and the way he could make her laugh. "No, I figured I could do things for you the fish couldn't, so I was pretty safe."

"True. Now on to the next issue. Santiago wants to ask Genevieve to stay here in Argentina. Evidently she's the only one who has been able to reach Miranda. The girl hasn't spoken to anyone in three months."

"Of course. The two of them seem to have really bonded. Maybe it's a shared trauma thing. Miranda is probably helping Genevieve as well. I can look after Max in Abu Dhabi; my father will also be there to help."

"And Jacques and Maya. They're heading back to Chile the day after tomorrow with Grand-Papa, but said they'd come to the race."

"I'm glad. I like Maya, but your brother scares me a little."

"Don't let Jacques intimidate you. He's a big softie." He turned her face up to his with a finger under her chin. "Are you ready to tell me what's bothering you?"

No! But he deserved to know. She'd already kept enough secrets from him. "Wesley was at the hotel yesterday when I returned from the track. He's given me an ultimatum: get back together with him or he'll fight me for custody of Max."

"You can't," Daniel blurted out. "You can't marry that bastard again. Tell me you're not even considering it."

"I have to consider it. My son will have a father and everything he could ever want in life. Wesley said I can go back to school, become a research scientist, and his family will fund my investigations into the neurological causes of food addictions. And I won't risk losing Max."

"What about us? I love you, Lexy. I can give you and Max everything Wesley offered and more."

She put her hands on either side of his face, drinking in the love in his green eyes. "We've had the most incredible two months together—beyond my wildest fantasies. But the adventure is ending and I have to face reality. What kind of life can we have together? The episode in Rio just proved that I can't drag Max around the world with us; his health is too precarious. And what about when he starts school? It'll kill me to stay at home while you race. God, I couldn't even do it in Rio. Not to mention the sheer stress of seeing you put your life on the line. I've had more binge eating relapses in two months than I had in four years. I need stability, Daniel. I need boring."

"I don't have all the answers right now, Lexy. But if we love each other, we'll find a way. Promise me you won't do anything rash."

"I told Wesley I'd give him my decision on December first." Already her heart felt like it was flatlining.

She had two weeks to come up with a solution. But hey, everyone loved a deadline.

***

The hot, dry Arabian wind blew across the track, making the car unpredictable. He'd already had two spins. But so had the rest of the field, so he was in good company. For the first time in years Daniel was looking forward to the end of the season. He just prayed he wouldn't be alone.

It had actually been hard to leave Argentina. They'd stayed five days, and each day his father had gotten a bit weaker, was awake fewer hours each day. Daniel had read the entire *Great Gatsby* book to him, although how much his father actually heard was anyone's guess. As they'd said goodbye, Daniel had had to wipe away the tears as he'd kissed his father's cheek and called him "Papa" for the first and probably last time.

Lexy had wept for an hour on the plane until she'd fallen asleep. Although she'd done her best to be upbeat for Max, Daniel knew the decision about their future weighed on her heavily. And every solution he'd been able to suggest still came with compromises—too many.

He was at the top of his career. One more win. It was the litany that had pushed him for the last five years. He couldn't imagine not racing. But neither could he imagine racing without Lexy at his side.

"Box, Daniel. We'll try for a few more runs when the wind dies down."

He headed back to his garage and climbed out of the car, which in the heat had turned into his personal sauna. Lexy was at the hotel with Max, so Daniel studied the telemetry and other data they'd managed to gather in his few successful runs. The Yas Marina circuit required complete concentration for the entire lap. Plus, as the race was run late in the afternoon and into evening, the lighting conditions were constantly changing. But with the two long straights, it was easier to pass with a fast car like his. Robert, however, had the same car beneath him and seemed to favor the night races, so it was anyone's guess who would take the championship.

By six o'clock they realized there would be no more running today, and he made his way back to the hotel. As Genevieve had stayed in Argentina, they were going to order room service rather than drag a jet-lagged Max out for dinner. Daniel was greeted at the hotel room by an ever-excited Max and a slightly worn-out Lexy. He felt like a real dad coming home after a day's work. His chest swelled.

He liked it. His family. For how much longer?

***

"Lexy, are you okay?" Maya's Canadian accent infiltrated Lexy's stupor. She was trying so hard not to think about food, it was all she could think of. A fully loaded hamburger and thick-cut fries were her current obsession. But she couldn't give in. Instead she forced another spoonful of plain, non-fat yogurt past her lips. Having dropped five pounds in the last two weeks, her skin hung off her even more. It was so disturbing she'd insisted the lights be off before she'd undress in front of Daniel. She was repulsing him, pushing him away, just like her mother had predicted.

"Sure, I'm fine. Where's Max? Is Jacques tired of him yet?" She searched the playground for her son, who was shouting encouragement to go higher on the swings as his pseudo-uncle pushed him. Despite there being no official relationship between her and Daniel, Max had started calling Jacques and Maya 'Uncle' and 'Aunty', much to their delight.

"No, Jacques loves him. It's good practice as well. He's both thrilled and terrified of becoming a father." Maya rubbed her still-flat belly.

"You're pregnant?"

"Yep. Just seven weeks, so there's ages to go yet. But we're excited. I'm kind of hoping this first one is a single to give us a chance to get used to having a baby. But my twin brother just found out that his wife is expecting twins. I haven't told Jacques. He freaks out enough as it is, making sure I'm eating properly. Who needs a pregnancy guide when you've got an overprotective husband?"

Lexy turned away at the look of love on Maya's face. *Why can't I have that without losing either my son or my sanity?* "Congratulations. I'm sure you'll be great parents no matter how many you have."

"Thanks. So what's up with you?"

"What do you mean?"

"You look like you're waiting for the other shoe to drop and crush you under it. What's the problem?"

"My time's up and I don't know what to do about it." Maya looked alarmed and Lexy hurried to explain. Well, sort of. The fewer people who knew about Wesley, the better. "Daniel and I, we agreed a short-term affair until the end of the race season. In forty-eight hours that will be over."

"Ah, I see. I thought that's what I was getting into with Jacques, just a casual affair. It's all fun and games until someone falls in love. Do you love Daniel?"

"Yes, more than I thought possible to love a man."

"So what's the problem?"

Even taking her ex-husband out of the equation, there was still no easy answer. "I don't deal well with stress. How can he cope with a girlfriend who falls apart on a regular basis when his very life depends on his being able to concentrate one-hundred percent on race day?"

"Oh, I see. Well, I'm not a shrink, so I'm not going to give you advice. But I will leave you with this question: Do you think maybe you're easily stressed because you haven't had the support of someone who loves you unconditionally? I was a wild child, lurching from one disaster to the next until I met Jacques. Now I get all the excitement and stimulation I crave from being with him. I'm a bit of a feminist, so I'm not going to say that Jacques completes me or anything. But he sure as hell fills in all the gaps and crevices so I'm able to function to my full capacity."

"Love isn't the issue. It's the rest of our lives that is complicated. I don't want to end up like my parents, having to choose between the well-being of my child and my marriage."

"Don't discount love, Lexy. It is amazingly powerful. But you have to believe in it and trust it with all your heart. Half a heart won't work." With that pronouncement, Maya strode off to join Jacques at the swing set.

"You're not going to the track for qualifying?" Lexy turned to find her father a few feet away.

"Papa, what really happened between you and Mum? Was I the reason you divorced?" Because even if she could figure out a way to keep custody, if things went wrong with Daniel, she didn't want Max to feel it was his fault.

"No, Alexandra, you were the reason we stayed together as long as we did. I don't want to put the blame entirely on your mother—after all, I was the one caught cheating. But your mother was raised in a gilded cage by her parents—always told how beautiful she was, so she thought that was all she had, her looks. And she was treated like a princess—everyone catered to her; she never had to deal with anything. When she became an adult, she had no coping mechanisms. If she didn't get exactly what she wanted when she wanted, she'd have a meltdown. In the end, I couldn't take it anymore and we separated. To save face, she told everyone it was because she wanted you to go to school and have stability."

"Do you think I'll end up like her?"

“Not a chance, *tesori*. You are strong. Just look at what you’ve overcome. And you’re raising an amazing son. You have made me so proud.” Her father wrapped his arms around her and hugged her tight. “Now, let’s go watch that man of yours drive.”

For the last time?

Chapter Seventeen

He'd done it. He'd actually, amazingly done it. He'd won. He was world champion. As he stood on the podium, listening to the national anthems, his eyes searched the crowd below. He'd managed a quick kiss with Lexy over the barrier as soon as he'd parked his car. Thousands of flashes had gone off, so no doubt that would be the cover shot on many newspapers tomorrow.

He scanned the faces again and spotted Jacques and Maya. But Lexy, her dad, and Max had disappeared. Maybe the crowds had been too much for her or Max and they'd meet him either in the garage, his trailer, or the hotel. He tamped down the disappointment. He'd wanted her beside him as he gave the informal interviews. As world champion it would be hours yet before he was released to celebrate his victory.

Eventually, he cornered his brother in the garage. "Where's Lexy?"

"She had to fly back to the UK. Her mother's had a heart attack and is in intensive care. Gian-Franco and Max have gone with her."

Suddenly he felt so tired he could barely stand. His chest was tight and it hurt to draw breath. "I would have gone with her. Is there any chance of catching her at the airport?"

"No. She left this for you." Jacques handed him an envelope with a pat on his shoulder. It was thick, more than just a quickly dashed note that said, "Got to go, be back soon." This was a tome spelling out the end of their relationship.

He slipped it inside his overalls where it sat heavy against his heart. "Thanks. I'll read it later."

When he'd won his first world championship, the victory party had lasted until four in the morning and he'd been photographed with no fewer than eight women. This one he left alone at ten thirty. He poured himself a whiskey while he stared at the letter from Lexy. He was on his second glass before he opened the damned thing.

My darling Daniel,

You are going to be so disappointed and you have every right to be. I should be standing before you, telling you this in person. But then you'd look at me with your beautiful eyes and you'd quirk up the corner of your lip the way you do, and I'd forget everything I want and need to say to you. So please forgive my cowardice in writing this letter.

First, I have to thank you for the two most amazing months of my life. You made me feel beautiful and special, things I never thought I'd be. You restored my faith in men and you taught me how a physical relationship should be between a man and woman. Although that lesson I have learned too well and don't believe anyone else will ever make me feel the way you do, so that's a bit of a bummer.

Second, I have to thank you for reuniting me with my father. And for letting me borrow your family for a while. You are truly blessed with people who love you. Don't ever let them go.

But, and you knew there'd be one, I have to do what's best for me and my son. I need a calm, quiet life where no one cares what Lexy Camparelli is wearing, or what she's eating, or who she's with. I can't fight my demons in public. But I'm not going back to Wesley. I'll figure something out. If I'm out of the media spotlight, maybe he'll forget we exist.

Daniel, you are an amazing driver. My father says you're one of the best he's ever seen. You have to keep racing. If you don't, if you give it up for me, you'll wake up one morning hating yourself, hating me. And trust me, I've been there, done that—it's not nice. I won't allow you to sacrifice your career for me. So don't try.

We had a great time. I hope that once the pain of our parting has dulled to an occasional ache, you'll be able to think fondly of me.

I love you with all my heart. And probably always will (double bummer).

Lexy

He scrunched up the letter and flung it into the corner before flopping onto the bed. It was over.

***

Lexy closed the flaps on the last box, sealed it with the packing tape, and wrote a note on the outside as to its contents. She wasn't supposed to lift anything heavy yet after her recent surgery so she left it for the movers. There were only a few things she was having shipped to her father's villa in Tuscany where she and Max were moving. The rest was going to an estate auction where the proceeds would be donated to Beat, the UK charity for eating disorders.

Her mother hadn't survived her heart attack and Lexy'd been too late to say goodbye. Not that she'd had anything really in mind. Perhaps, "I forgive you," but as her mother had never accepted any responsibility for the part she'd played in Lexy's obesity, that probably would have fallen on deaf ears. At least her mother was at peace now. Lexy made sure the obituary notice had included a photo of her mother at her most beautiful, and had made mention only of her retiring from modeling to live a quiet life with her daughter.

Lexy, Max, and Papa had attended the funeral. How empty a life her mother had led to have only three people grieve her passing. But it rammed home to Lexy that she had to make different choices. She had to take risks and be strong and fight for what she wanted. Who she wanted. She wanted Daniel. Being without him these past weeks had been hell.

"Mummy, Mummy, when are we going to see Andrew?" Max ran into the room, followed more slowly by her father.

"In just a few minutes. Did you put the presents for him and his new baby sister in the car?"

“Yes. Mummy, when can I get a baby sister?”

“Not for a while yet, sweetie.” Maybe never. Daniel hadn’t tried to contact her or see her since her departure. She’d wanted to properly kiss him goodbye, but the call about her mother had prevented that. It was probably a good thing, because she wasn’t sure how she’d have let him go in person. Maya had phoned and reamed Lexy out for breaking up by letter. But she’d also been supportive when Lexy had explained about her eating disorder. That was one thing Lexy’s therapist had suggested, telling others so they could help. She didn’t have to do this alone anymore. She had family and she had friends.

Even better, she had leverage. In cleaning out her mother’s house, she’d found a box of papers that had set her free. She’d completely forgotten that when she’d packed up the house she’d lived in during her brief marriage, she’d stored a few boxes of stuff to go through later at her mum’s. In addition to the uncashed check for a million dollars were some rather incriminating documents against her ex-husband and his father, the contents of which she’d threatened to leak to the press if he made any claims on her son. Wouldn’t the world love to know that the “charitable” donation the Hardings had made to the college in Cambridge had actually been to guarantee that Wesley graduated top of his class? With just a token protest, he’d promised to never contact her in the future. Marrying her again had obviously not been his idea. One day she’d have to tell Max about his father, and it wasn’t a conversation she looked forward to having.

But if she could fill his life with good male role models, hopefully her son would get over having a loser as his sperm donor.

Her father put his arm around her as she took one last look around her mother's house. There weren't many happy memories, and she'd be glad to never see it again. "Are you ready to go?" he asked.

"Yes, Papa."

"Then the van driver wants to check the destination address with you one last time."

"Can't you tell him? It's your house we're going to."

"Evidently, as your name is on the contract, you have to be the one to speak with him. I'll take Max down to the beach." Her father and son both disappeared so fast it was like it was prearranged. What was going on?

Lexy rubbed her dusty palms on her jeans and wandered out to the front of the house. A tall man wearing the dark overalls of the moving company lounged against her father's car. He reminded her so much of Daniel that for a second she had to close her eyes while the pain in her chest eased.

"Are you ready to start your new life?"

Damn, it even sounded like Daniel. Too much. Her eyes flew open, and before she could stop herself she was in his arms.

"Daniel, what are you doing here? And why are you dressed like a removals man?"

"Just assessing my career options. The other choice is driving instructor, seeing as how I did such a fabulous job teaching you. I'm guessing from the shiny 'L' on the back of this car that you passed your learner's test."

She leaned back on his arm. "What do you mean, career options? You've got at least ten years left in F1, you told me yourself. And you're the current world champion, so you can't quit now."

"Go out while you're on top, they say. And as much as I love driving, I love you more. If you need a quiet life away from the media spotlight, then that's what we'll live."

"You can't give up Formula 1 for me. You'll regret it and end up resenting me."

He kissed her then. The mastery of his lips, so familiar but still exciting, left her breathless. "I've spent the last five weeks missing you more than I can bear. The thought of never driving again pains me less than not waking up next to you every day for the rest of my life."

"There has to be some compromise we can reach." She was going to fight for this. They'd find a way.

"So you'll come back to me?" His face was so earnest she reached up and caressed his cheek.

"I never really left you. You've been in my heart this whole time."

"What about Wesley? Has he filed for custody? We can disappear like Jacques and Maya, if necessary."

She shook her head. "I've sorted that out. I'll tell you about it later. I can't believe you'd give up your life for me."

He shrugged. "It was kind of a no-brainer, as I

didn't have much of a life without you."

"Maya gave me some amazing advice, but I was too afraid to take it. She said if you trust completely in love, it can work miracles or something like that. Let's trust that we'll be happy."

"Already there, *cherie*. Now, your father said he would keep Max occupied for an hour. Have all the beds been packed away already?"

"Not all. And I've got a surprise for you." She pulled him into the house, to her old bedroom, the scene of so many tears. It would be fabulous to leave a happy memory here. She stripped off her clothes, pleased to see Daniel disrobe as quickly. He reached for her then stopped.

"What have you done?" He seemed afraid to touch her.

"Just a minor procedure." She'd had a modified tummy tuck and her skin was tight again. She'd never be thin, but she was happy.

"You didn't need to do this for me."

"I love you, but I didn't do it for you. I did it for me. I want to rock a bikini at the pools of all those swanky hotels you stay at. I want to feel great about my body so that when I have a bad day I can take off my clothes and see how far I've come."

"Then it's my job to make sure you never question your beauty or how much you mean to me."

She put her hands on his face and drew his head down to hers. "Enough talking. We have a championship to celebrate. How many times do you think you can 'box' before my father and Max come back?”

“I’m going for quality over quantity. Besides, I didn’t tell Gian-Franco I’m quitting F1. Instead, I made a deal with him: If I could convince you to marry me, I’d consider driving for Ferrari when my Mercedes contract is done. So, I’m going to pretend I’m still a driver and I’ve switched teams and now have to learn to take things slow.”

She laughed. “He’ll kill you if he hears you say that.”

“Ah, but if I’m in your arms, I’d die a happy man.”

“I’d really rather you didn’t die at all.”

“Whatever my love wishes.”

“I am so going to quote you on that. But maybe you’d better get a start on convincing me to marry you.”

He reached for her then and it was like coming home.

If home was where the heart is, then hers was in his arms.

Epilogue

Lexy pinched herself to make sure she wasn't dreaming. She had everything she'd ever wanted and more. Her new family sat at the dinner table, laughter flowing as readily as the wine. Daniel was next to her, his arm along the back of her chair. Max sat on her left and Papa was next to Daniel's Grand-Papa. Jacques and Maya completed the set, making everyone feel as though the house was theirs as well. Marie and the rest of the staff seemed ecstatic to have the family enlarged and back in residence.

Next month the house would be even fuller when Santiago, Genevieve, and Miranda came for a visit from Argentina. Lexy had been surprised to hear that her friend and Max's former nanny had married Daniel's half brother within a month of starting to work for him. She looked forward to hearing the story behind that whirlwind romance.

A shaft of light from the chandelier sparkled on Lexy's huge engagement ring. It hadn't taken Daniel the full hour to convince her to marry him. Even better, they'd worked out a compromise for the next two years at least. Daniel was going to continue to drive and when he raced in countries where they didn't feel comfortable taking Max, then her son would stay with Maya and Jacques. Maya said she'd need all the hands she could get to help with the twins she was expecting. When Max started school they'd reevaluate. And in the meantime, Lexy was going to continue her psychology studies without having to worry about working and paying bills. Problems would undoubtedly come up. But she knew that as long as they trusted in their love, they'd make the right decisions.

"Daniel, when you marry my mummy, can I call you Daddy? Andrew let me borrow his daddy, but I'd like one of my own."

"Absolutely, Max. In fact, if you don't want to wait, you can call me Daddy now." They'd talked about this and were prepared for the question.

"Can I drive your boo-cat-ee?" That one they hadn't discussed.

"Ah, no."

"Oh, well. *Nonno* said I could drive his Ferrari," Max announced.

Papa choked on his wine. "I said when you get older you can drive *for* Ferrari."

Everyone at the table laughed. Her heart swelled. She never imagined she could be this happy.

And this was just the beginning.

****

Thank you for reading *The Playboy and The Single Mum*. Please post a review where you purchased the book. Your opinion will not only help other readers decide whether to buy the book or not, it will also help me continue to write the stories that I, and hopefully you, love to read. Thank you!

Read Santiago and Genevieve's story in:

The Tycoon and The Teacher

He'll do everything he can to avoid love. It may not be enough.

Argentinian tycoon, Santiago Alvarez recently lost his sister, brother-in-law, and father. Now he's solely responsible for his traumatized niece, Miranda, who hasn't spoken for three months. His only hope to help Miranda recover is a woman who tempts him like no other. Whatever it takes, he'll live up to his promise to care for his sister's daughter—even if it means marriage.

French teacher Genevieve Dubois is slowly recovering from post-traumatic stress disorder after the death of a student. Her new position, helping a little girl find joy again, brings with it an unusual complication—a super-sexy uncle who awakens Genevieve's desire for a family of her own. When her employer proposes marriage so he can keep custody of Miranda, Genevieve accepts, hoping to turn their passion into love. But when she discovers the real reason Santiago wants to be guardian of his niece, it threatens all their futures.

The Tycoon and The Teacher

Chapter One

Genevieve glanced at the man beside her. *Mon Dieu, what have I gotten myself into?* The lure of a child in distress had really landed her in a mess this time.

The car sped past miles of vineyards; the snow-capped peaks of the Andes Mountains stood tall and proud like sentinels guarding Argentina's Mendoza valley. It wasn't being so far from her home in the Loire region of France that had unnerved her, though. It was the man next to her in the back seat. Santiago Alvarez was about as gorgeous as men came. His dark brown hair was swept back off his face, and his strong jaw and Roman nose matched his starched and stiff demeanor. Yet all he'd had to say was that his eight-year-old niece hadn't spoken in the three months since her parents died—could Genevieve come and see if she could do anything to help?

And here she was.

The added push, of course, was that in three weeks her current position watching over little Max Castellioni was coming to an end. And the thought of returning to teach in a classroom still sent her heart rate into triple digits. Another job, one on one with a child, was what she needed to stay sane … to keep from remembering.

"Could you tell me about your niece before I meet her?" Genevieve asked. The silence had become as awkward as the time she'd asked a student's mother when her baby was due, only to be told she wasn't pregnant.

"Miranda's eight, and her parents died three months ago," he replied.

That was the best he could do? The child had been living with him since August. Maybe he wasn't used to interviewing nannies. Or being quizzed by them. "What does she like to do?"

"I don't know. I think she likes princesses. As I mentioned, she hasn't talked in three months, not even to me."

"But you knew her before her tragedy, didn't you? What was she like then?"

His hazel eyes clouded for a moment as his gaze lingered on her face. Then he resumed staring at his phone. "Like most eight-year-old girls, I imagine. I'm not very good with children."

She forced back a huff of frustration. Poor child, no wonder she hadn't spoken with her uncle, who was doing an impressive impersonation of a stuck-up jackass. *He's dealing with his own grief. Be gentle.* Genevieve pulled in a deep breath and released it slowly. "Okay, tell me about her parents then. Were they happy? What kind of family life did they have?"

"Beatriz and Denman were the perfect couple. They loved each other so much, it was a mercy they were taken together."

Not if it meant leaving their daughter orphaned, surely. But Santiago seemed to think death preferable to living without someone he loved. No way was she going to try to find the water in that well.

Best to keep the conversation on Miranda's parents. "How did they meet?"

"Through me. Beatriz is … was my sister." He paused for a moment and swallowed. "I went to school with Denman and we became friends first, then business partners. I don't think Denman stood a chance once Beatriz decided he was what she wanted."

"And does Miranda take after her mother or her father?"

"Probably more Denman."

She tilted her head to the side, taking advantage of Santiago's distraction with his phone to linger in her gaze. He really was gorgeous. His lips were full, and when he'd smiled once at something Max had said, they lifted up, slightly crooked. His long fingers gripped his mobile device like it was a life raft in a storm-tossed sea. But she wasn't about to be so easily dismissed, not when a child's happiness was at stake. "Denman doesn't sound like an Argentinian name."

"His mother was English, his father Argentinian. Miranda's last name is Suarez. And she speaks and understands English if you don't speak Spanish."

"I can get by," Genevieve responded. No need for

him to know about what happened in Honduras.

The vehicle pulled up in front of an elegant Mediterranean-style villa. The plaster's soft yellow glowed against the backdrop of the setting sun. The house was surrounded by a large garden, but beyond that, as far as the eye could see, were grapevines. It was a stunning place— too bad it currently held so much unhappiness.

"Welcome to my home," Santiago said as she scrambled out of the car before he or the driver could come around and open her door. He stood so close, his intoxicating scent enveloped her. "As we say in Spanish, *mi casa es su casa*."

My house is your house. *I wish. Beats my small, drab apartment any day.*

"Thank you." Before she could say more, they were surrounded by the rest of Santiago's guests. They'd all flown from Rio de Janeiro in his private plane but had taken two separate cars from the airport to his house. Only Daniel, Santiago's half brother and the reason they were all together, had stayed in Brazil to compete in his Formula 1 race.

"Shall I take Max?" Genevieve held her arms up to the little boy, who usually came willingly. She was, after all, paid to care for him.

"Don't worry, Genevieve," Lexy, Max's mother, said. "I'll look after Max tonight. Why don't you meet Santiago's niece?"

Genevieve forced a smile. She'd hoped for at least a few minutes' break from her host's company.

"My staff will show you to your rooms," he said, gesturing towards the steps, atop which stood three uniformed maids. "When you're ready we can meet on the back veranda for drinks before dinner."

Genevieve thought a large whiskey might be needed to cope with the diverse personalities in the crowd that had converged at the hospital when Max had an asthma attack a few hours earlier. Santiago had the good luck to pick that moment to arrive in Rio to convince his newfound half brother Daniel to come to Mendoza to meet their dying father. If that weren't complicated enough, Daniel's other half brother, Jacques, and his wife, Maya, had also shown up, almost giddy with the freedom of coming out of hiding following the death of the crime boss Maya had testified against.

And now the family reunion had decamped to Santiago's place to give Max time to recover and to wait for Daniel to finish the next race. How a group of blood-related strangers planned to get along under one roof she had no idea, and she didn't really want to get involved. In fact, Lexy and Daniel had given her the option of staying in Rio and she'd decided to do just that.

Until Santiago had told her about his niece.

Genevieve climbed the steps beside Santiago, who waved away the other maid as they approached. "Thank you, Magdalena," he said. "I will show *Señorita* Dubois to her room."

Genevieve shot him a glance. Why did she deserve such personal attention? Aside from his request regarding his niece, he'd barely said ten words to her. Even when they'd returned to the Rio hotel to grab the luggage, he'd spent the entire time on his phone, conducting business. Perhaps her room was in the staff section or near his niece. Daniel and his girlfriend Lexy had never treated her like an employee, so she wasn't quite sure where she stood now. Was she invited to drinks and dinner, or expected to get her meal in the kitchen with the other staff?

Santiago led her down a long, wide hallway. Every five meters stood a small table with a large vase of fresh flowers that filled the air with their exotic perfume. Near the end of the hallway he opened a double set of doors, revealing a large room complete with fireplace, sofa, and a gorgeous sleigh bed. This was no staff accommodation.

"I hope you find this room satisfactory."

"It's beautiful. But very grand. Are you sure this is for me?"

"Yes, I asked the housekeeper to get it ready for you especially."

"Okay." She drew the word out, waiting for her brain to process what her eyes were seeing. Was this some game he was playing? Give her the best room and then expect something from her in return? She'd seen the way he looked at her when he thought she was distracted. Did he think she'd be wowed by luxury and fall at his feet? She'd grown up playing in Jacques's huge chateau where her aunt was the housekeeper, and she traveled around the world on her current job, always staying in the best hotels. Luxury was nothing new.

More enticing was the lure of Santiago's strong arms wrapped around her, snuggling against his broad chest, making her feel safe… She shook her head to clear that image from her mind before it had the chance to take root. Time to get back to the real reason she was in his house. "Would you like me to meet your niece now?"

"When you're ready." His gaze roamed over her again, and she could feel the heat rise in her cheeks. Had he caught her staring at his chest? *Dieu*, he must work out regularly.

She needed a minute for a reality check. While she was hot and bothered, the man in question was cold enough to warrant a frostbite warning. Why was she suddenly thinking about being in his arms? Her father had taught her to look after herself. She didn't need a man to keep her safe.

The scars on her back begged to differ.

"Fifteen minutes. Where shall I meet you?"

"I'll come collect you." He closed the door gently behind him and she pulled in a deep breath. Hopefully, she would spend the majority of her time with Max and Santiago's niece. Because too much time near him and she'd be a mess. Having grown up on various army bases, she was used to authoritative, muscled men. Her reaction to Santiago was out of character. Which made it worse. She had no idea how to deal with it.

Maybe some fresh air was what she needed. She opened the doors at the far side of the room. A two-meter wide terrace ran half the width of the house. The sun had just dipped below the horizon, leaving a blaze of orange and pink–hued glory in its wake. Genevieve was about to step out when the patio doors next to hers flung open and Santiago emerged. What? He'd put her in the room next to his, with a shared balcony? She retreated to her room, but only to the point where he couldn't see her unless he turned around, although she could still see him. His jacket and tie were off, and he'd rolled his sleeves up. Casual, but just as sexy.

At first he leaned his forearms on the stone railing, staring at the sunset. Then he scrubbed his hands over his face as though exhausted, and bowed his head between his arms. He looked like a weary man carrying the weight of the world on his shoulders. She resisted the urge to go to him, run her hands over his back, and ease some of his tension. He stayed like that for a minute more before straightening and returning to his room.

She glanced at her watch—five minutes left to get ready. While she'd been staring at her host, someone had slipped her suitcase in her room. She pulled out a long, Bohemian-style skirt that was meant to be wrinkled and a caftan top and changed into them. Hurriedly, she ran a brush through her hair, leaving it loose. She hadn't yet found her flat shoes when there was a knock on the door.

Barefoot, she opened the door. Santiago had switched his shirt and ditched the tie but still wore a suit. His gaze roamed over her and a warm, crooked smile lit his features. He seemed about to touch her hair but pulled his hand through his own instead. That second of humanity was quickly replaced by another cool, detached expression.

"Do you need more time?"

"Just to find my shoes. I threw everything in my bag and didn't pack properly, as we were in a hurry."

He glanced down at her feet, and she stopped herself from wiggling her toes. "Miranda hates shoes and refuses to wear them most of the time." It was the first personal insight he'd given about his niece.

"I like her already. I'll stay barefoot, then. It will give us something in common."

He hesitated a moment, his gaze returning to her feet, then turned and led her back downstairs and along the hallway to a room at the far end. After knocking softly, he opened the door. The room was bright and cheery and huge. But not cozy. Her eyes scanned the room, looking for Santiago's niece. A matronly woman sat on a chair, wearing what Genevieve assumed was the uniform for some exclusive nanny company. Opposite her, huddled in a tiny ball, was a dark-haired girl, pristinely garbed in a school uniform, except that her toes peeked out from under the hem of her dress. The nanny put down the book she'd been reading and peered at Santiago over the rim of her glasses.

"*Señor* Alvarez, I didn't expect to see you tonight. I thought you would be with your guests."

"Thank you, Marta. You may take your dinner break now. *Señorita* Dubois and I will spend some time with Miranda."

Miranda didn't raise her chin from where it rested on her knees. Marta put the book down and whooshed out of the room without even saying "bye" to the child.

"Miranda, *Señorita* Dubois has come to visit for a few days," Santiago began.

No response from the little girl. He shifted his weight from one foot to the other. He probably addressed heads of state without a qualm. But it looked like an eight-year-old girl had him baffled.

Dieu, the man had no idea how to relate to his own niece. He wasn't even trying. Miranda continued to stare at the floor, shredding Genevieve's heart. When Santiago made no move to get closer to the little girl, Genevieve turned to him, wanting him to read the anger in her eyes. "You may go. I'll stay with her. And will you tell Lexy that, if she wants, Max can take his supper in here with us?"

His eyes widened. "I don't allow eating in the bedrooms."

Although she wanted to tell him where he could shove his rules, she tried for a diplomatic approach first. Miranda needed peace, love and reassurance, not an angry tirade. Genevieve put a hand on Santiago's arm but quickly dropped it. "Please, can we eat in here? It's been quite a day and I'm not up to a big dinner."

His eyes searched hers, questioning her actions. But she couldn't get the little girl to open up to her with her pole-shoved-up-his-ass-I-don't-allow-eating-in-the-bedrooms uncle around.

"Very well. I'll have your dinners brought here."

He looked around the room. "I'm sure we have a portable table—"

"No need. We'll eat on the floor."

"What?"

"Trust me, Santiago."

It was the first time she'd used his name, and it rolled off her tongue with more passion than she'd intended. It sounded more like a caress than a command. And judging by the way his eyes flared, he'd noticed it as well. *Merde*, having personal fantasies about the way his body would feel molded to hers was one thing, but letting him know she'd thought about it was another.

"Very well. I'll check on you after dinner."

"Quick question. Has Miranda cried much?"

"Not at all as far as I'm aware. She hasn't said a word since I told her of her parents' passing."

"Okay. See you later."

He obviously wasn't used to being dismissed, as he stood there for several more seconds while she went over to the bed, grabbed as many pillows and stuffed animals as she could, and proceeded to plop down on the floor in front of Miranda. Finally, the door closed behind him.

After settling herself on a pile of cushions, Genevieve picked up a toy rabbit, and using a funny voice said, "Genevieve is such a long name. I can hardly say it." She nodded the rabbit's head as if it were speaking.

"I know," Genevieve responded. "What was my mother thinking? But my little friend Max calls me

Vivi, and I quite like it. You can call me Vivi, too."

"Okay, Vivi," the rabbit pretended to say.

"What's your name?" Genevieve asked the toy.

"Albert."

Miranda shook her head but didn't say anything.

"You don't look like an Albert," Genevieve continued. "I think you are Patrice."

Again Miranda shook her head.

"Bertrand?" she tried again. This time the little girl raised her head before shaking it.

"How about Esteban? Esteban the rabbit. That must be it," Genevieve said with a note of triumph in her voice.

"Peter," a soft voice said.

Not wanting to scare Miranda, Genevieve pretended it had been the rabbit that gave its name. "Of course, Peter Rabbit. How could I have forgotten? Is Jemima Puddle Duck here, too, somewhere?"

Miranda slid off her chair and, with a toe, pointed at a small stuffed duck. A child schooled in the classics. Excellent.

Genevieve continued a silly conversation between herself, the stuffed rabbit and the duck. A tiny smile appeared on Miranda's face for a second before disappearing. Poor child was so stuck in grief she felt guilty for a simple smile.

Just as Genevieve's throat was getting sore from so much talking, the door opened and Max hurtled through in his usual boisterous manner. He'd quickly recovered from his trip to the hospital earlier in the day.

Lexy stood by the door. "Are you sure?" she asked as Max dived onto the pile of pillows. Miranda was now sitting on the floor, although she still had her knees drawn up to her chest. But at least she'd raised her head. Until Lexy had arrived—and then it was back to her fetal position.

"I'm sure," Genevieve responded. "Enjoy your dinner. I'll come get you if there are any issues."

Lexy nodded and closed the door behind her.

"Miranda, this is my friend Max. Except he's so bouncy I think he should be called Tigger." On cue, Max jumped to his feet and bounced around the room, yelling, "Boing, boing, boing" as he went. Miranda stared at him in a mix of amusement and astonishment.

Genevieve grabbed up the book the nanny had left. "Max, come sit down. I'm going to read a story." She didn't want his *boinging* to bring on another asthma attack.

Instantly, Max was in her lap, ready to be read to. He snuggled into her arms and stuck his thumb in his mouth. Genevieve opened up the book—*Gulliver's Travels*, in Spanish. Not what she'd have chosen for an eight-year-old, but if Miranda liked it…

She began to read, her Spanish a little rusty after almost a year. After the third paragraph, Max protested. "I can't understand any of it. Are you talking Italian like my *nonno*?"

"No, *petit chou*, it's Spanish, Miranda's language. Just listen for now. You can tell what's happening from the pictures, and I'll explain in a minute."

But before she could resume reading, Miranda got

to her feet, went across to a bookshelf, and pulled out another book. She handed it to Genevieve before sitting again. Except this time the little girl sat right next to her. Tentatively, Genevieve lifted her arm and put it around Miranda. Although she sat stiffly, Miranda didn't protest at the contact. Another victory.

The book was a Winnie the Pooh story in English. Genevieve read it slowly, pointing out things in the pictures, trying to get Miranda to join in with Max's running commentary. She still hadn't said a word, aside from "Peter," but now the stuffed rabbit sat in the little girl's lap as the three of them cuddled.

By the time Santiago and Lexy returned, the two children were in their pajamas and Genevieve snuggled with them on the huge bed. Max was valiantly trying to stay awake but didn't protest when his mother lifted him into her arms to take him to her room.

"Everything okay? Where's Marta?" Santiago asked, his gaze searching both Miranda and Genevieve's faces.

"Just fine. I told Marta she could have the night off, and that I'd stay with the children." The older woman had been horrified to walk in while Genevieve and the children were eating their dinner in their laps, seated on the floor. Miranda had instantly stiffened again and started to withdraw, so Genevieve sent the nanny away.

"You're here as my guest, not an employee," Santiago said.

"Then as your guest I'm asking you to give Marta

the rest of the week off and allow me to spend time with Miranda. We have a lot in common, don't we, *petit chou*?" Genevieve wriggled her bare toes as she waited for Santiago to respond.

Santiago stared at her as if trying to see into her soul. *I wouldn't peer in there; it's pretty dark at the moment.* Finally, he gave a curt nod. "If that is what you wish."

"It is."

"Would you have a drink with me on the terrace off your room after Miranda goes to bed?"

"If that is what you wish." She repeated his stilted reply and was rewarded with a slight lifting of his lips. *Dieu*, if the man were any more rigid he'd be a statue with pigeons perching on his head.

"Goodnight, Miranda. Sleep well."

Santiago left and Genevieve shook her head. She was going to show the man what a precious gift his niece was if it took everything in her.

Now, she just needed to keep the darkness at bay long enough to show him the light.

~~~~~~~~~~

Get your copy of The Tycoon and The Teacher today!
~~~~~~~~~~

Also in the Vintage Love series:

The Vintner and The Vixen

It's all fun and games until someone falls in love.

Maya Tessier needs a fresh start after her last boyfriend dragged her deep into an organized crime ring, putting her life in danger. After inheriting a cottage and acreage in France from her great-grandmother, she hopes to escape her turbulent past to concentrate on her art. Unfortunately, her inheritance is within the estate of a privacy-obsessed billionaire. And he wants it all back.

Jacques de Launay has led a life of rigid control, working hard to repair the family's fortunes after his playboy father nearly destroyed them. His one attempt at happiness ended in tragedy when his pregnant wife was killed in a car crash. He'd rather be the last in the illustrious de Launay family line than open himself up to that kind of heartache again. Then Maya Tessier arrives on his doorstep and he discovers it's not only the ancestral land he wants to reclaim.

But if he lets her stay, more than his heart may be at risk.

Visit www.alexia-adams.com to read an excerpt.

The Developer and The Diva

Para siempre means forever. That's what they'd promised one another. Then she left.

Now she's back, and *para siempre* is just two words written on the wall of the community center he's determined to tear down … and she wants to save.

Eduardo Forenza's property development project hits a snag when a protest committee recruits a celebrity to head up their cause. But the Argentinian developer grew up on the rough streets of La Boca—he's not going to be intimidated by some big shot who's never felt the cold bite of hunger. When the star who stands in his way turns out to be the same woman who ripped out his heart and used it to fuel her rise to fame, he's determined to purge her from his system once and for all. If only he didn't have to keep rescuing her first.

Anna Marquez is known to the world as the singing sensation Angel. Launched into stardom by an avaricious mother, Anna had to leave everything behind, including the man she's never stopped loving. Now she's back in Buenos Aires to bury her beloved grandmother and solve an intimate dilemma. But when her personal problem is overshadowed by attempts on her life, Anna flees to the one place she feels safe: Eduardo's arms.

Will the pain of the past be too much to overcome, or will they gamble again on a love to last *para siempre*?

Thank you, Reader

I hope you enjoyed reading Daniel and Lexy's story as much as I enjoyed writing it. If you did, please help other readers find it by leaving a review at your favorite retailer. It doesn't have to be long but your opinion matters to me and other readers.

If you'd like to find out about other books in the Vintage Love series, upcoming releases, contests, and events, please sign up for my monthly newsletter at https://alexia-adams.com.

You can also get in touch with me via my website (https://alexia-adams.com) or follow me on Facebook (https://www.facebook.com/AlexiaAdamsAuthor) or Twitter (https://twitter.com/AlexiaAdamsAuth).

I love to hear from readers, so don't be shy.

About the Author

Alexia Adams was born in British Columbia, Canada and travelled throughout North America as a child. After high school, she spent three months in Panama before moving to Dunedin, New Zealand for a year where she studied French and Russian at Otago University.

Back in Canada, she worked building fire engines until she'd saved enough for a round-the-world ticket. She travelled throughout Australasia before settling in London—the perfect place to indulge her love of history and travel. For four years she lived and travelled throughout Europe before returning to her homeland. On the way back to Canada she stopped in Egypt, Jordan, Israel, India, Nepal, and of course, Australia and New Zealand. She lived again in Canada for one year before the lure of Europe and easy travel was too great and she returned to the UK.

Marriage and the birth of two babies later, she moved back to Canada to raise her children with her British husband. Two more children were born in Canada and her travel wings were well and truly clipped. Firmly rooted in the life of a stay-at-home mom, or trophy wife as she prefers to be called, she turned to writing to exercise her mind, travelling vicariously through her romance novels.

Her stories reflect her love of travel and feature locations as diverse as the wind-swept prairies of Canada to hot and humid cities in Asia.

To discover other books written by Alexia or read her blog on inspirational destinations please visit: www.alexia-adams.com or follow her on social media.

Other Books by Alexia:

Love in Translation series:

Thailand with the Tycoon

Will being trapped in a failing resort change more than their itinerary? When his older brother suffers a heart-attack, Caleb is sucked back into the family's virtually bankrupt hotel business. He reluctantly travels to Thailand to evaluate a last-chance resort with the help of a translator. Getting stranded with an enchanting local was not on the agenda. Neither was falling in love.

Visit www.alexia-adams.com to read an excerpt.

Bali with the Billionaire

He's all business. Until she makes him her business. Ever since tragedy shattered Harrison Mackenzie's life, he's locked his passion away to focus on work. Until a captivating woman without boundaries crashes through his meticulously constructed barriers to reach the billionaire's broken heart. Is he finally ready to risk loving again?.

Visit www.alexia-adams.com to read an excerpt.

Guide to Love series:

Miss Guided

Mystery writer Marcus Sullivan is determined find someone for his younger brother Liam. Playing matchmaker on holiday in St. Lucia, Marcus tries to interest Liam in a beautiful local tour guide Crescentia St. Ives. Then Marcus gets stranded with Crescentia and the plot to match her with his brother quickly incinerates in the flames of lust. No way can Liam have her when Marcus can't keep his hands off. Too bad he can't write a happier ending to their blossoming romance.

Visit www.alexia-adams.com to read an excerpt.

Played by the Billionaire

Internet security billionaire, Liam Manning, made a promise to his beloved brother, Marcus, to complete his mystery-romance manuscript. Problem is that Liam's experience with women is limited to the cold-hearted supermodels he usually dates. So falling back on his hacking skills, he infiltrates an online dating site to find a suitable woman to teach him about romance—regular guy style. What he didn't expect was for the feelings to be so … real. Can Liam finish the novel before Lorelei discovers his deceptions and, more critically, before she breaches the firewall around his heart?

Visit www.alexia-adams.com to read an excerpt.

His Billion-Dollar Dilemma

Simon Lamont is an ice-cold corporate pirate. But when he arrives in San Francisco to acquire a floundering company and is accosted by a cute engineer with fire in her eyes, it takes all Simon has to maintain his legendary cool. Helen will do whatever it takes to change his mind, and if that means becoming the sexy woman Simon didn't know he wanted, so be it. If only she wasn't about to walk into her own trap...

Visit www.alexia-adams.com to read an excerpt.

Masquerading with the Billionaire

World-renowned jewelry designer Remington Wolfe is competing for the commission of a lifetime and someone is trying to destroy his company from the inside. He's in for more than one surprise when his unexpected rescuer turns out to be a sexy computer specialist with a sharp tongue and even sharper mind.

Visit www.alexia-adams.com to read an excerpt.

Romance and Intrigue in the Greek Islands:

The Greek's Stowaway Bride

Hoping to make it to North Africa to free her uncle, Egyptian heiress Rania Ghalli stows away on the yacht of Greek millionaire Demetri Christodoulou. But when Egyptian agents board the boat, she can either jump overboard … or claim she's Demetri's new bride. Demetri needs a wife to complete a land purchase so he agrees to play along—if she'll agree to a real marriage.

But keeping the vivacious heiress out of his heart will be a lot harder than keeping her on his ship…

Visit www.alexia-adams.com to read an excerpt.

Romance in the Canadian Prairie:

Her Faux Fiancé

Take one fake engagement to a man she once loved, stir in a very real pregnancy, add a marriage of convenience, bake in the heat of revenge and you get the mess that has become Analise's life.

Visit www.alexia-adams.com to read an excerpt.

An Inconvenient Series:

An Inconvenient Love

With the Italian economy in ruins, Luca Castellioni can't afford a distraction from running his successful property restoration company. However, he needs an English speaking wife to cement a crucial deal. When his British bride-of-convenience undermines the foundations around his heart, he's forced to restructure his priorities. Is he too late for love?

Visit www.alexia-adams.com to read an excerpt.

An Inconvenient Desire

Investment banker Jonathan Davis retreats to his Italian villa to lick his wounds following his divorce, so his flirtation with runway model Olivia Chapman is just that. But when his ex-wife dumps their toddler daughter on his doorstep, Olivia's assistance is a godsend that shakes up his world in more ways than one.

Visit www.alexia-adams.com to read an excerpt.

Business Trip Romance

Singapore Fling

Lalita Evans's father hired Jeremy Lakewood in the family's international conglomerate, and now he's tagging along as she oversees their interests across eight countries in three weeks. Will Jeremy risk his livelihood and all the success he's achieved to win the woman who haunts his dreams?

Visit www.alexia-adams.com to read an excerpt.

Daring to Love Again Series:

The Sicilian's Forgotten Wife

Bella Vanni has accepted that her presumed-dead husband is long gone, so it's a huge shock when he knocks on her door and announces his desire to resume their marriage. She can't trust his answers on where he's been or why he left, and she certainly isn't keen to walk away from the life she's constructed for herself in his absence. But when Matteo's freedom is threatened, Bella must decide which is most important to her: everything she's painstakingly built or a second chance at a love that never died.

Visit www.alexia-adams.com to read an excerpt.

www.ingramcontent.com/pod-product-compliance
Lightning Source LLC
LaVergne TN
LVHW020707110826
845149LV00012B/2143

* 9 7 8 1 9 9 9 1 7 5 6 9 6 *